Browsing for Trouble

Amy E. Lilly

DEDICATION

To my husband , Dennis, for his enduring faith and
support of me when I tell him crazy plotlines or lock
myself in my writing room for hours on end . Thank
you for bringing me tea with honey or coffee fixed
just the way I like it . Thank you for being my biggest
fan.

ACKNOWLEDGMENTS

Thank you to Shari Flynn for my cover. I have no artistic skill and am always amazed by her ability to turn my idea into art. Thank you to my beta reader and best friend Maricruz Baker. She gets me and Phee.

CHAPTER ONE

"No men and no murder," Juliet declared as she lifted her glass in the air. "This girls' vacation will be margaritas, mojitos and manicures."

"You won't get any argument from me," I said, clinking my margarita glass to hers. "It was awesome of Willow's parents to let us stay here for free. I plan on relaxing by the pool, reading the latest mysteries from my favorite authors and catching up on my sleep."

"Uh…can anyone say boring?" Juliet pretended to stifle a yawn. "You can read anywhere, and you can sleep when you get back home. This vacation is all about fun, and the sun, and spending time with your soon-to-be married baby sister."

"The sun makes me freckle and what I suggested is fun."

"Wear sunscreen, for Pete's sake. What are you? Ninety?" Juliet complained. "I've created a list of all the things I want to do while we're here in Sedona. I want to go on one of the Jeep trips through the desert, go hiking, and go see the place where gravity doesn't exist-"

"Gravity always exists here on Earth. There's no way it can't exist. If it didn't exist, we would weigh ten pounds and float," I said with a skeptical look.

"Look!" Juliet thrust a guidebook under my nose. I grabbed it from her.

"It's called an energy vortex." My eyes skimmed through the description. "People come from all over the world on vision quests or missions to feel the energy. Hmm…this sounds right up you and Willow's alley. A bunch of woo woo healing and crystals. Have fun with that. I'll be in the spa getting a massage." I put my sunglasses on and took another sip of my margarita. I lay back on my chair and let the sun sprout another freckle on my nose.

"Dang it, Flea! You promised we would have a real girls' vacation before Wade and I get married. This is my last bit of freedom before I settle down, clean house, and make babies one day." She snatched the guidebook back and glared at me.

"Fine. I'll go to the healing crystal woo woo vortex if you promise to go with me to some of the museums."

"Deal." Juliet grinned. "This is gonna be the best trip ever!"

"Well, before I get blisters on my feet hiking in the desert, I plan on getting pampered. It's time for our mud bath."

"Willow said her parents don't like to call them mud baths. They're restorative body treatments. I signed us up for the Prickly Pear Garnet treatment. It's supposed to make your skin soft and silky smooth. Plus, it pulls out all the toxins and bad mojo with the stones they place around you."

"If they can keep me from having any more murder mojo, I'll declare this trip a success. My skin is already soft and silky smooth," I said. I sipped the last of my margarita and stood up to head indoors to the spa.

"That's not what Clint said," Juliet snickered. "He told me to make sure you get buffed and bedazzled and to make sure someone takes care of those horse hooves you call feet."

"What?" I cried. "Look at these toes. These are the feet of a movie star." I showed her my short, fat feet with the pearly pink toenails.

"If you're a hobbit." Juliet laughed. "I'm just kidding. Clint just told me to make sure you had fun. He worries about you, Phee."

"I know he does," I said softly. "I'm okay. I worry about Nellie Jo. She seems so sad now that Mike's gone. He was her whole world, and now, she has to figure out how to live without him."

"Nellie is tougher than you think. Did you know she's signed up for yoga and a college class?"

"No. Really?"

"Yep. She told me she's going to try all the things she was too scared to do before. She said each time she does something new, she can hear his voice in her head telling her she is being a nervous Nellie. It makes her smile."

"I'm glad," I said. "We should all try new

things even if they make us nervous."

"Um…yeah…didn't I just say we needed to go to the vortex? Hello? New. Different." Juliet gave me an incredulous look.

"And we are." I pulled open the door to the room where Juliet and I were scheduled for our spa treatments. A woman was lying on the table with clay covering her arms and face. The rest of her was covered by a white sheet. "Oh! I'm sorry. I thought our appointment was at two o'clock." She didn't move or even acknowledge we had entered the room.

"Maybe she's deaf," Juliet whispered.

"If she's deaf, why are you whispering?" I hissed back. "Ma'am? Is your aesthetician here? I think there's been a mix up in times."

The woman still didn't move. I moved in closer and noticed that she did not appear to be breathing. "Ma'am? Are you okay?" I asked in a loud, clear voice. I turned to Juliet. "She might be asleep."

Juliet stepped forward and shook the woman to awaken her. As she did, the woman's arm fell off and clattered to the floor.

Juliet screamed and shattered the quiet tranquility of the spa. "Oh, my goddess! Oh, my goddess! It's some kind of horrible flesh-eating zombie disease and now I've got it! I've got the plague. I'm gonna lose my arms and my teeth. I'm not going to be able to wear my sleeveless wedding dress because I won't have any arms!"

She hopped around the room flapping her hands and squawking like a hen in heat.

In shock, I looked at the woman who still hadn't moved. It was then that I noticed something strange about her mud-covered body. I leaned down and picked her arm off the floor and thrust it towards Juliet.

"What in the blue blazes are you doing, Phee?" Juliet screeched. "Now you've got the plague! Poor Mom and Dad will be heartbroken!"

"It's not real," I said. I tried to hand her the arm, but she just shook her head and backed away from me in fright.

After a moment, Juliet calmed down enough to ask, "So it's a prosthetic? Is she...dead?"

"Not quite, Jul. What we have here, my dear hysterical sister, is a mannequin. Someone just played a very nasty trick on us."

CHAPTER TWO

"I'm so sorry," Willow's mom, Harmony, said for the third time. She twisted a large turquoise ring nervously around on her finger. "I can't imagine someone wanting to play such a horrible prank."

"We're okay," I said. I reached out and patted Harmony on her shoulder. "Personally, I thought Juls was hilarious squealing about how she was going to turn into a flesh-eating zombie."

Juliet shot me a glare. "I didn't think I was going to turn into an actual zombie. I was worried I had caught some kind flesh-eating bacteria. It was hyperbole. It's what we artistic souls do."

"This is getting out of hand," Steve said. Willow's father, Steve, was as different from Harmony as I was from Juliet. His blue polo shirt and neatly pressed khaki shorts contrasted sharply with Harmony's flowing tie-dyed skirt, multiple rings on her fingers and toes, and long gray braids.

"Hush, Honey Bear," Harmony said.

I gave Juliet a wide-eyed look and mouthed, "Honey Bear?" She snickered then quickly tried to cover it with a cough.

"These girls are Willow's friends, so that makes them family as far as the spirits are concerned, Sugar Plum. We may as well tell them. Willow did say that they are civilian police back in Miller's Cove."

What the heck had Willow been telling her parents about Juliet and me? Civilian police? Try neighborhood watch, and only if I remembered to stay awake long enough to stick my head outside and look up and down the block. Sure, we'd solved a crime or two, but it was more sheer luck and stupidity than my mad detecting and library skills. Despite reading every Nancy Drew and Agatha Christie novel ever published, most of the information I'd gleaned had not come in handy when I was confronted by a gun-toting, alligator-loving criminal.

Harmony gave a long, drawn out sigh. "You're right. We need some kind of help because that bumbling buffoon of a deputy the sheriff sent out last time isn't going to help us out."

"This isn't the first so-called joke that's been played on some of our guests. At first, we thought that it was just the spirits being playful, but Harmony said it was humans at work, not my spirit guides trying to get our attention."

"I can see where Willow gets her...uh...connection to the other realm," I said. "What kinds of things have been happening?"

"Guests' personal belongings have been taken from the dressing rooms and put in odd places like the dining room. A huge scorpion was found in a chafing dish on the breakfast buffet. Just little things." Harmony shrugged. "To be honest, we weren't too worried until it started happening more frequently, and we started to lose business.

I'm not in this for my health. I've got a bottom line to meet and business partners who like to see a profit at the end of each quarter."

I raised my eyebrows. Despite her hippie looks, Harmony seemed to be a hard-nosed business woman. I wondered what Steve's role was in the business. Perhaps he oversaw channeling the spirits for guests of the resort.

"I assume you've talked to all of your staff. There aren't any disgruntled former employees or dissatisfied customers with a grudge?" Juliet asked.

"Steve, didn't want to upset the staff by interrogating them," Harmony said dryly. Her fingers tapped out a nervous staccato.

"Most of them have been with us since the beginning. They're family," Steve protested and grabbed Harmony's hand to calm her.

"I've been to some pretty testy family reunions and holiday dinners myself," Juliet joked. "Sometimes family can surprise you."

"I was twelve, and it was only mashed potatoes. You flicked a pea at me first!"

"As I was saying," Juliet continued, "you should probably still ask the staff if they know of anyone who would play these kinds of tricks on guests. Perhaps they know something you don't."

"Do you have any rivals? Enemies?" I asked.

"I don't think so," Steve said, but I detected a bit of a hesitation in his voice.

"Are you sure?" I pushed gently. "Everybody

at one time or another has made somebody angry."

"Well ..." Steve began.

"Oh, for heaven's sake, Steve! They'll hear about it from Willow eventually, so we might as well tell them!" Harmony snapped. She took a deep breath and closed her eyes. "Sorry, Honey Bear. You know how much all of this upsets me."

Steve grabbed her hand and pulled it to his mouth and kissed it. "It's okay. The spirits and I see your true heart. We know it's worry, not anger, that makes your aura turn red."

Oh, sweet honeyed jalapenos, it was like being around a male version of Willow. I hoped I wouldn't be required to interrogate the spirits to get a straight answer from Steve.

"Harmonious Healing Spa and Resort was built on sacred ground," Harmony blurted out. "There. I said it. It's not really a secret, but we don't tell guests about it either. Many of our resort guests come here to get in touch with their sacred energy. If they thought that we had built their spiritual retreat on a sacred site...well, we'd be in the red before week's end. Some of our more...uh, spiritual guests don't like to see the ancestors disturbed. Personally, I think it's a crock of-"

"We didn't know when we built the spa," Steve interrupted her. "It came to our attention about a year ago that our realtor may have been less than forthcoming with us regarding the history of the property."

"May have? The woman is a thief and a liar!"

"What do you mean by sacred site?" Juliet asked. "Isn't most of the land around Sedona sacred?"

"The Yavapai tribe believe that Sedona is where the tribe was born. According to an ancient legend, Kamalpukwia is the first woman and they all came from her. Idelia said that the tribe considers this land where the spa sits as part of the area where Kamalpukwia emerged from the earth."

"Idelia?"

"Idelia Riggs. She is a council woman for the Yavapai tribe. I'm not really sure what exactly she does," Steve said.

"She's in cahoots with that reprobate realtor, is what she is!" Harmony spat. "I'm sure they have some kind of scheme they're pulling. I don't trust her or Francine. Francine is the realtor from Sun Vortex Realty who sold us the land. Now she's been skulking around here saying the tribe's willing to pay us the original sales price for the land. Like that would even put a dent in what we've spent on constructing the hotel and spa."

"How long ago did you build the spa?" I asked.

"We broke ground two years ago. The spa's been open for about a year."

"Francine would be the first person I would question if I were the police," Juliet said.

"The deputy who came to investigate the first time is Francine's brother," Steve said with a woeful shake of his head.

"Hmm…is there anyone else that might have a reason to want the resort to fail?" I asked.

"No. Francine and Idelia are the only two I can think of, and honestly, I don't know how either one of them could have done it," Harmony said.

We heard someone walking down the hallway towards the office where we sat. A moment later, the door flew open and a short woman with long, dark dreadlocks peeking out from a floppy turquoise hat walked in.

"Mummy! Daddy! I'm home!" Willow announced happily.

CHAPTER THREE

"Willow! What are you doing here? I thought you wouldn't get here for another two days," I said. Willow refused to fly with Juliet and me to Arizona. She said the spirits and birds were the only creatures allowed to fly. She planned to take her Jeep across the country in a four-day driving marathon from Miller's Cove to Sedona. "Did you break down and get on a plane?"

"Not in this lifetime. If the spirits wanted me to fly-"

"They would have given you wings. We know," I interrupted. "How did you get here in two days?"

"The spirits gave me help."

The door burst open again. Lu stood in the doorway with her face red and sweaty from carrying two suitcases. "You know you could've stayed and helped carry these. What the heck did you pack? Books?"

"Stones."

"What the freak?" Lu sputtered. "Rocks? You packed rocks. We're in the ever-loving desert surrounded by a million red rocks, and you packed rocks?"

"No," Willow said calmly. "I packed stones. Healing stones and crystals. My spirit guides told me they were needed."

Lu dropped the bags on the ground and collapsed on top of one. "It's hot, I'm tired, and I got rocks in my butt from sitting in that old jalopy you call a Jeep for the past twenty-four or more hours."

"What are you doing here, Lu? I thought you weren't going to be able to get time off for our girls' getaway?"

"Juls, where there's a will, there's a way. Once Willow started spouting about how the spirits were warning of danger in the desert, Clint insisted I come with her to keep an eye on Phee."

"Clint doesn't even believe in Willow's spirit guides," I said.

Willow gave me a pitying look and shook her head. "Just because he doesn't believe in them, doesn't mean the spirits aren't there. I told him the spirits' message and he brushed off my concerns. The next day he called me and asked me if Lu could go with me to keep an eye on you and Juliet. Clearly, the spirits visited him in his sleep and changed his mind."

Harmony stepped forward and pulled Willow into a hug. "I'm thrilled to have you home early, whatever the reason."

Willow hugged her mom for a minute. Once she extracted herself, Willow said, "So what exactly is going on here and why are the spirits clamoring for my attention?"

"You just got here. There's time enough for all the negative vibes later," Steve protested. He grabbed Willow's and Lu's suitcases. "Let's get you two settled into rooms and we'll talk over dinner. Phee and Juliet need a little rest and relaxation themselves after all the day's commotion."

Steve headed out of the room towards the hotel portion of the resort. Willow and Lu followed behind him bickering quietly over who did the most driving on their road trip.

"I guess we'd better get out of these robes and into some real clothes," Juliet said.

"I feel terrible you girls missed your restorative treatments," Harmony said. "Let me call down to the spa and see if Marianne can fit you into her schedule."

"You don't need to do that," I said.

Juls kicked me and gave me a look that told me to be quiet.

"I insist. This is supposed to be a relaxing week for the bride-to-be and her friends. You will enjoy your time at the spa even if I have to do the treatments myself."

Harmony picked up the phone and after a brief conversation with the person on the other end, she hung up and smiled. "There. You two head on down to the spa. Marianne and Sandy have no appointments until later today, so she can just squeeze you in."

I thanked her, and Juliet and I walked to the spa area. "Juls, were you raised by wolves? We didn't need to have her go out of her way to do this. For heaven's sake, we are paying a fraction of the cost for this vacation anyway, so-"

"I want to question the aesthetician," Juliet interrupted me. "I don't care about the mud wrap, Flea. Who has the most access to that room? Unlike you, I'm already on the case."

"I've created a monster," I groaned. "I thought after our alligator debacle, we decided to give up on crime. As a matter of fact, I'm so over solving crimes, I actually checked out a bonnet-ripper romance to read."

"I thought they were called bodice-rippers."

"They are, but this is a romance set in Amish country. I don't think they wear bodices, so I figured when things get racy the heroines ripped off their bonnets. I'm a new woman. My life is all love, sewing my own clothes and ripping off my bonnet for Clint. No more crime."

"You're full of manure," Juliet laughed. "You hate romance books, you love a challenge, and mystery is in your blood. Come on. You know you're dying to know what's going on here."

"Not really," I lied.

We went back to the room where the armless mannequin had been. A young woman with long blonde hair waited for us.

"Ladies," she said. "I'm Marianne. So sorry about the little snafu earlier." She gave a gapped-tooth smile of apology. "One of you will be with me. Sandy will take care of the other treatment."

"I'm Phee and this is my sister, Juliet. I'll go with Sandy," I offered.

"Head to the room next door and she'll be

right with you. If you both want to change into these paper underwear, Sandy and I will start your treatment sessions in five minutes." Marianne handed Juliet and I small folded squares and stepped out of the room.

I unfolded the paper to reveal a paper thong the texture of a paper hospital gown. "What in the world am I going to do with this? That won't even cover one cheek!"

"It's to give you some modesty. They paint mud on your rear end, too."

"Oh heck no. I'm not having mud on my backside. It's as soft and smooth as playdoh already."

Juliet gave me an exasperated look. "We're girls. They're girls. Get over it and just go get muddy." She shooed me away.

I headed next door to a room like Juliet's. Soft music composed of water and flutes piped in from a hidden speaker. The lights were dimmed to a twilight glow. I ignored my discomfort and removed my robe and swimsuit and donned my paper thong. No matter which way I tugged it, only a half inch of my rear end was covered. Giving up, I lay down on the table and pulled the white sheet up to my chin. I closed my eyes and tried to relax.

There was a light knock on the door and a moment later, I heard it open.

"Are you ready?" Sandy asked.

"Yes," I squeaked and pulled the sheet even

tighter to my paper-covered flesh.

A petite woman with short-cropped dark hair came into the room. She looked like a pixie with her sharp, gamine features and large dark eyes. "I'm Sandy and you must be Willow's friend, Phee. We're doing a cleansing treatment today, correct?"

"Yes," I squeaked again. I cleared my throat and repeated. "Yes. I'm a little nervous."

"No need to be nervous. This is a very relaxing treatment that will release all the toxins in your body and clear away the negativity that is keeping you from realizing your true potential."

"Mud can do that?"

"It's not just any mud. It's mud from the womb of Kamalpukwia. It's sacred mud from far out in the desert that we bring here for our guests. It's not only good for your body, but it's a cure for what ails your soul."

"That's some potent mud," I joked nervously. "Are the ancestors okay with you putting it on people's bodies?"

Sandy tugged the sheet gently from my hands. "Certainly. We all originate from Mother Earth. Here at Harmonious Healing, we reconnect our guests with their roots. Our goal is to ensure that you leave here enlightened and at peace with your world. Now, if you could roll over, I'll start with your back."

I rolled over. Sandy began to paint mud onto my back. It was warm and had the loamy scent of the earth after a hard rain.

"Have you worked here for very long?" I asked. If I was going to be practically naked in front of a stranger, I wanted to at least know a little about her.

"Since they opened. Harmony and Steve are great."

"Did you hear about my run-in with the practical joker?"

"Yes," Sandy said. "I hope whoever is doing these horrible things stops soon. It's not good for business." Her brush strokes became a little more aggressive as she spoke.

"I wonder who would want to hurt the business." Dang it. Juliet was right. I did want to find out what was going on. I comforted myself with the fact that there was no murder.

"Not me," Sandy said. "I take care of my mom and little sister. I need this job."

"I heard there was a little bit of controversy because of where the spa was built."

Sandy gave a snort of disgust. "In Sedona, every square inch of land is a sacred site. I'm part Yavapai and I don't remember anything sacred here. If Idelia had her way, every inch of the desert would be declared sacred to our ancestors."

"Maybe it's a disgruntled old employee."

"Possibly," Sandy said hesitantly.

"Anyone leave here unhappy with Steve and Harmony?"

"Just one guy. I think his name was Brad or maybe it was Chad. I don't remember. It was a few months back. He's got some tie to Marianne. It's her ex or something. I don't really hang out with anyone else. Between work, helping my mom and night classes at the community college, I barely have time to sleep, let alone socialize. I just know he didn't work here very long before he was asked to leave."

My librarian senses were tingling. "Do you know if Brad or Chad still has keys and access to the building?"

"Oh, I don't know." Sandy must have realized she had said too much because her voice had changed. I might be Willow's friend, but I was still a guest. "I never really knew him more than to say hello in the hallway. Can you roll over now? It's time to detox your front."

Closing my eyes and willing myself not to blush, I rolled over onto my back. Juliet owed me two museum visits after this and a visit to the local library. So far, this girls' retreat had not been relaxing at all.

CHAPTER FOUR

An hour later, I was showered and dressed in a turquoise sundress and espadrilles. Sandy had offered no additional information during our session and after she had laid stones from my forehead to my navel, she had suggested that the detox would work better in silence. I was hoping Juliet had better luck prying information from Marianne.

I wandered down to the dining room to wait for everyone. As I rounded the corner, I heard raised voices. I could see outside on to the patio through the large windows to my right. I spotted a tall man with his hair pulled back into a man bun shaking his finger in Marianne's face. Her face looked to be carved out of granite and as his face reddened in anger, hers grew cooler. I couldn't quite make out what was said over the background music of flowing water and flutes, but it was not a friendly conversation.

"What's up, Flea?" Lu said from behind me.

Startled, I jumped and let out a loud squeak of surprise. It must have been loud enough to be heard outside because when I looked back out the window, the man was gone and Marianne was walking away from the building towards the parking lot.

"You're quieter than a mongoose looking for a cobra," I complained.

"It's what makes me a good cop. Cop by day.

Sneaky ninja mongoose warrior by night."

I rolled my eyes. "Or it could be that I was preoccupied with the two people arguing outside. One of them could be behind all the trouble the spa is having. It was a tall guy with a man bun. That alone should be grounds for arresting him. Worst fashion statement ever."

"What trouble?" Lu said. "You mean Willow's spirit guides were actually right? Is there danger in the desert?"

"What are you two talking about?" Willow asked. She had come downstairs in a pair of faded blue jeans and a t-shirt that read *I brake for good "car"ma* with a picture of a VW beetle beneath it.

I debated on whether I should tell Willow what had been going on at her parents' resort or let them break the news that someone didn't wish good karma on the spa guests. After a moment's hesitation, I decided against saying anything.

"I think," I said slowly, not meeting Willow's gaze, "that my belly is in rebellion against the tofu and green bean salad that I had for lunch. I hope there's something with a little more protein and calories for dinner."

"The chef is excellent," Willow said. "She moved here from Vermont to pursue her passion for vegetarian cuisine in a supportive environment. Kathy is devoted to incorporating the herbs and edible desert plants into the menu."

"But she does include meat for the guests, doesn't she?" I said hopefully.

"Of course not." Willow dashed my hopes against the dining room floor's red tiles then stepped on them as she added, "Tonight she's prepared a prickly pear gelato for dessert. It's so yummy that it makes the spirits wish they were corporeal so they could taste it."

"I'll give them mine to eat," I grumbled under my breath. If I was lucky, I could convince Juliet and Lu to head out to Sedona later that evening to hunt down a hamburger or even a french fry.

Juliet bounced down the stairs on her long, tanned legs, and I decided french fries should remain off my menu for at least another five pounds or so. Once again, I wondered if I'd been adopted or perhaps a hobbit foundling. My parents could have been hiking in the woods when they found me as a baby hobbit with fat, hairy feet and decided to take me home to raise as their own. I was short and slightly rounded in my proportions while my sister was tall and lean. I looked at a carrot and gained two pounds. She could eat a box of cookies and never gain an ounce. I felt a twinge of guilt for my moment of envy.

"I am super excited to try the cactus gelato tonight!" Juliet gushed to Willow.

My moment of guilt was over, and I gave her dagger blows with my eyes. "I'm going to tackle a lizard and roast it over the barbecue to get some meat in my system," I groused.

"Ew. Phee, you always get grumpy when

you're hungry. Let's go have a glass of wine and some dinner, and I can tell you everything I learned from Marianne."

We sat down at the nearest table in the small, intimate dining room. It contained only ten tables, but from what Willow had said, the tables stayed booked during the peak tourist season.

"Something's going on here," Willow said. "I know it. The spirits know it, and I can tell you two know it. Spill it!"

I sighed. "It's nothing big, Willow. Someone's been playing some mean jokes on the guests here. Juliet and I were the latest victims of the prankster."

Harmony and Steve joined us at the table and after the waiter had brought everyone drinks, the discussion resumed.

"Why didn't you tell me all of this?" Willow asked her mother. "Have you called the police? Grilled the staff? Done a cosmic cleansing?"

"No, no, and yes. Your father ran around here chanting with sage and lavender. The place stank for days afterwards. It's not a big deal. Just a couple of tricks played on guests. No one was hurt. It's just irritating. Personally, I think it's Francine. The woman is sneaky and dishonest."

"Now, Honey Bear, you don't know that. You can't accuse people of negative things otherwise it may come back to bite you in your karmic butt," Steve said with a serene smile on his face. By the look on his face and his laidback attitude, I

25

thought Steve may have been burning more than just sage and lavender.

"Phee and I are on the job," Juliet announced, not meeting my eyes. "We're going to get to the bottom of this if it kills us."

"Hopefully not!" I squeaked. Dang it! I promised myself I would steer clear of crime. Hang up my magnifying glass and stick to books. Now, she had just shanghaied me into helping find out who was behind the shenanigans.

"Thank you. I'm sure it's just some local kids who Francine hired to make our lives difficult. She found a buyer who will pay premium dollars for this location and we won't sell. I guess she figures if our business gets too bad, we'll be forced to sell at a lower price. Well, I'm not a quitter!" Harmony's hand came down on the table so hard it made our silverware jump.

Fortunately, our first course arrived and relieved the tension and silence that followed Harmony's outburst. I was relieved to see it was a salad made up of a mixture of greens and heirloom tomatoes. No tofu topping, thank goodness, but no crunchy croutons either.

I leaned over to Juliet and hissed, "Thanks for talking to me first before offering us up to investigate."

Juliet smirked and whispered, "I know you questioned Sandy. It's in your blood. You carried a junior detective kit before you carried a lunchbox, so you have to find out what's going on. So, what did you find out?"

That's the problem with sisters. They know you better than anyone else. "There is a disgruntled employee named Brad or Chad. She wouldn't tell me why he was fired and she changed the subject after that so I couldn't find out anything else."

Lu eyed us suspiciously. "What are you two whispering about down there? Juliet looks like the proverbial cat in the cream."

"There was a disgruntled employee who might be behind all of this. What can you tell us about Brad or Chad and why he left?" I asked Harmony. I knew better than to ask Steve because he had a pair of rose-colored glasses view of the world and its inhabitants.

"Brad Cassidy. He was flirting with some of the female guests and he was caught with a female staff member in the buff, so I fired him. From what I heard, he headed towards the west coast to look for a new job."

"Can we talk about something else?" Steve complained. "All this negativity is turning my aura gray."

"Daddy, you're not gray. Just a little tinge of blue around the edges," Willow said.

The main course arrived and the talk around the table turned to Juliet's upcoming wedding.

"It's going to be so awesome to get married under the full moon," Juliet practically clapped her hands in glee.

"I'm just glad I get to wear shoes during all of this. The last thing I need is to step on a snake during the ceremony," I grumbled. "I like shoes. I have shoes for every occasion, but for some reason my sister wants to get married barefoot by the lake."

"It's so Wade and I will be connected and in tune to the earth, water and sky. We want nothing between us and our new beginning."

"I'm surprised we're not going to be doing this wedding in the nude," I said.

"Well, I proposed it, but Mom shot the idea down faster than a rattlesnake strikes its prey."

"I think it's beautiful," Steve said, tears glistening in his eyes.

"It is beautiful," I agreed, "that my mother insisted on clothes."

"Amen, sister!" Lu raised her water glass in agreement. "Last thing I want to do is see my partner and boss buck naked. Back in New York, we like to keep as many layers between us and the mass of humanity as possible."

We concentrated on eating the vegetable concoction in front of us. I recognized a carrot and possibly something from the bean family, but anyone's guess was as good as mine on the ingredients. It tasted good even with no meat, so at least I wouldn't starve.

After dinner, Steve and Harmony mingled with the guests occupying the other tables. There were two blue-haired ladies from Phoenix visiting for the week, a couple traveling across the country on their honeymoon who planned to stay a few days, and a middle-aged physician and his wife, who was a geologist doing research in the hills surrounding Sedona.

While we were enjoying our pear cactus dessert concoction, a young woman hurried over to Harmony and whispered in her ear. Harmony grabbed Steve's hand, and they both rushed out of the dining room into the kitchen.

"Something's up," Willow said. "My father doesn't move that fast unless he's trying to buy Grateful Dead tickets." She stood up and followed her parents.

"Are we just going to sit here?" Juliet asked.

"It might be nothing. A failed recipe. A mouse in the polenta. Not everything is mysterious, you know." I was curious, too, but I had promised myself and Clint that I would not investigate anything else after the alligator nearly ate me for an appetizer. I had gone back to being an armchair sleuth, and I was okay with it. Kind of. Not really. Curse you, Nancy Drew! "Oh, heck! I can't stand it. Let's go find out what's going on."

"Yes!" Juliet bounced up out of her chair.

Juliet and I followed Willow out of the dining room. Lu gave up on her dessert and trailed after us. As we walked through the swinging doors into the kitchen, I could see that everyone was gathered around the walk-in deep freezer.

"What's going on?" I asked Willow.

Willow stepped back, and I looked into the freezer. A man lay sprawled face down over a large white bucket with a knife sticking out of his back.

"Aw, crap on a cracker. It's another darn murder!" So much for my promise.

CHAPTER FIVE

"Everybody step back," Lu commanded in her work voice. "I'm law enforcement even if this isn't my jurisdiction. I'm sure the local sheriff won't want you guys trampling over the evidence."

We all backed away from the body in the back of the freezer. Despite the warmth of the evening, after the cold of the walk-in and the shock of seeing a body with a knife sticking out of its back, a shiver ran through me.

"Poor Brad," the waitress from earlier sobbed. She buried her head into the chef's shoulder.

So, this was the disgruntled employee, Brad Cassidy. I guess I could go ahead and strike him off the suspect list.

"It's alright, Bridget," Steve said in a soothing voice. "Why don't you go on home."

"Sorry, sir," Lu said. "I'm sure the sheriff is going to want to talk to everyone here. Has someone called nine-one-one yet?"

"I did." The chef raised her hand like a student in the classroom.

"And you are?"

"Kathy Whitestone, ma'am. I'm the chef here at the resort."

It was always surprising to see Lu in her role as deputy sheriff. She was so sarcastic when she was off-duty, but the minute the bodies hit the ground and murder was in the air, she became an investigating machine. She was no longer Lu, she was Deputy Gifford. She exuded authority and confidence, and people recognized it.

"So that was Brad. Someone just eliminated our primary suspect," Juliet whispered.

"Not really," I said. "He could still have been the prankster. The murder could be totally unrelated."

"You going to tell Clint we found another body?" Juliet asked.

"Oh, heck no. Besides that, I didn't find a body. Chef Whitestone found a body. I'm just an innocent tourist here to enjoy a girls' getaway with my sister. I don't know anything, I didn't see anything, and I'm not involved in anything."

"Right," Juliet drawled. "And my name is Santa and I have a house at the North Pole I want to sell you."

"Why don't we all move back into the dining room. Law enforcement should be here any minute and they'll need to get in here. I would appreciate it if no one would say anything to the other guests." Harmony began to usher us from the kitchen back into the dining room.

"I don't think we'll be able to keep the guests from finding out about this, Mom. Police will have to talk to all the staff and probably the guests, too. They'll have an ambulance and all sorts of people here." Willow clung to her father's arm. Worry washed over her normally calm face.

"I know. I just…I just-" Harmony burst into tears. Steve and Willow hurried to embrace her as sobs racked her thin frame. I turned away to allow the family some privacy.

"This bites," Juliet said quietly. "I'm sorry I dragged you to the desert and dead bodies."

"Like you could have predicted this. Not even Willow's spirit guides saw this one coming."

"Untrue."

I jumped and practically piddled myself. Was that a spirit guide talking to me? I realized after a moment that it was Willow. She had left her parents to come stand with Juliet and me.

"The spirits told me that something was happening here. Why do you think they urged me to talk to Clint?"

I sighed. No matter how I hard I fought it, Willow's spirit guides and woo woo magic always seemed to poke its way into my life. Despite my better judgment, I had to ask. "Did the spirits warn you that Brad was going to be murdered?"

"Not in those exact words. If they had, I would have prevented his death. They told me that a negative aura surrounded my parents' business and someone wished them great harm. Clearly, a murder on the premises isn't going to help their business."

"We have to find out who has a grudge against your mom and dad," Juliet said.

"My parents are the coolest people. They

volunteer their time at both the homeless shelter and the animal shelter. They donate money to all sorts of causes. My mom is on committees, and my dad helps troubled kids by taking them on vision quests in the desert. Who would want to be mean to them?"

"It might not be personal, Willow. It may be someone who doesn't like the resort being here, or Brad made someone angry and this has nothing to do with your parents."

"I wish I could believe that, Phee, but first a bunch of pranks are played on guests driving away their business and now a corpse was found in their couscous. I think someone has a lot of negative energy, and it's all pointed at Mom and Dad."

Two deputies arrived. Fortunately, the other dinner guests had finished their dinners and the dining room was empty except for us.

"Good evening. I'm Deputy Cramer and this is Deputy McCall. We got a call about a possible murder here."

"Oh, I think it's more than a possibility," I said. "The victim has a knife sticking out of his back. Plus, he was found in the back of the kitchen's freezer."

"Your name?" Deputy McCall asked.

"Phee, I mean, Ophelia Jefferson. This is my sister, Juliet. We're guests here."

Steve stepped forward. "Buddy, it's good to see you. I've got to say I wish it was under better circumstances."

"Me, too, Steve. What's going on here?" Deputy Buddy McCall asked.

Steve gestured for the two officers to follow him. Harmony and Willow trailed behind them. Although I wanted to follow and listen in on the scene investigation, I restrained myself. I had to physically restrain Juliet because she started walking towards the kitchen until I grabbed her arm.

"I want to know what's going on," she complained.

"I'm sure Lu will give us skinny when they're done in there. Slow your investigative roll, Starsky."

She plopped down on a nearby chair. "Our girls' getaway is turning into a big old flop. This is a sign from the spirits about the chances of my marriage succeeding."

"Baloney! Don't try weaseling out of getting married because of a dead body or two."

"I have to wonder if the spirits are sending me a warning."

"The spirits are too busy talking to Willow and Steve to worry about your marriage. Besides, if Wade caught wind of a spirit guide messing with his marriage plans, he'd blast them to kingdom come with his shotgun."

"He doesn't believe in guns."

"He was in the Marines. Of course he believes in guns."

"Not anymore. I've changed his ways. He's all about karmic bliss and yoga. He even agreed to try meditation."

"Oh, good golly. He's probably napping, not meditating."

Lu walked out of the kitchen. Her mouth was a grim line and her face looked hard.

"Those two," she jerked her thumb towards the kitchen, "are pinheads."

"What's wrong?" I asked.

"They gave me a load of crap for sticking my nose into another state's crime scene. Next time I'll let people traipse all over every last bit of evidence and if those two yokels can't solve the crime, then too bad, so sad."

"First, there won't be a next time because I'm over dead bodies. Second, no you won't. You're too good of an officer. Crime busting is your super power."

"Well, I guess they don't like a girl putting her high heels in their case."

"You wear heels?" Juliet tried to joke, but Lu glared at her.

"Of course not. They're horrible for your feet. I meant that those two chuckleheads probably have a problem with females in law enforcement."

"They better not, or I'll bust their butts all the way to Tucson," a female voice drawled. An older Hispanic woman stepped from the doorway into the room. "Alicia Martinez. I'm the sheriff of

Yavapai County."

"Deputy Gifford from Miller's Cove," Lu said as she shook the sheriff's hand.

"Glad we had you on site, Deputy. We don't get very many murders here in Sedona, but it helps to have a clean crime scene to work."

"Glad I could help, ma'am. I can't promise it was pristine since the chef and the owners walked into the deep freezer to view the body after the waitress found the victim, but I did my best."

"It happens. What can you tell me about the victim?"

"Not much. Seems he was a former employee here at the spa by the name of Brad Cassidy. He was fired a few months back, and according to everyone here, they all thought he'd moved out of state."

"Well, I'll go check with my deputies and see what else they may have learned. The coroner will be here in a few minutes. I passed him on the highway a few minutes ago. That man drives slower than my ninety-year old grandma. Good thing the dead don't mind the wait." Sheriff Martinez laughed at her own gallows humor. She tipped her hat at us and walked into the kitchen.

We all stood there awkwardly, unsure of what to do next. I heard humming from Juliet. After a moment, I realized she was humming a song from the movie, *Frozen*.

"Are you serious? Do you really think the song *Do You Want to Build a Snowman* is appropriate?"

"I can't help it. It's in my head, and I can't get it out." Juliet cocked her head sideways and shook it like a dog fresh out of a bath. "Nope. Still there."

Lu snorted. "There is only one good thing about this whole mess."

"What's that?" I asked.

"You two don't have your bedazzled crime-fighting masks with you."

CHAPTER SIX

"I'm putting Willow on the payroll." Clint's voice came in fits and starts as the spa's internet connection tried to handle the video call back home to Miller's Cove.

"Maybe her spirit guides anyway." I chuckled. Clint's face was a little distorted since the connection was not the best. Even so, his smile made my heart thump a little harder in my chest.

"I am not going to be an ogre," Clint promised. "I said I was trainable, and I am, but it's taking every bit of my self-control to keep from hopping the next flight down there."

"I know," I said softly. "At least I have Lu."

"She's a good cop, but she can't hug you and kiss you like I can."

"I hope not! I like Lu, but I draw the line at public displays of affection with her."

"I really want some private display of affections with you right now," Clint growled which made me giggle.

"I'll be back in a week," I promised. "It gives you just enough time to miss me."

"I missed you two seconds after you walked out of the door."

"I love you," I said and touched my fingers to the computer screen in a vain attempt to feel the warmth of his face.

"I love you, too, Ophelia Jefferson. Promise me you'll be careful and come back in one piece."

"I promise."

We said our goodbyes and disconnected. I shut the lid of my laptop. Things were good with Clint. He and Watson had moved in with Ferdinand, Fritz and me. The transition had been easy for the two of us, and the pets had reached some kind of compromise. Ferdinand ruled the house and the dogs stayed out of his way. It worked and peace reigned for now. Clint had rented his aunt's house to Nellie's son and daughter-in-law. They had recently returned from overseas. The family needed a place to stay, and Nellie needed her family close after Mike's murder. It was the perfect solution while they looked for a home to buy for their growing family.

Clint hadn't asked me to stay away from the investigation. He knew me well enough to know that any attempt on his part to stop my curiosity made it grow even stronger. I was uneasy though. Juliet and I weren't home in Miller's Cove. Out here in the desert, the red cliffs, which were so beautiful at a distance, contained danger that you couldn't always see. Could they also hide the motive behind all of the problems here?

I was too tired to think about anything else. I stretched out on the bed and tried to read the Tony Hillerman mystery paperback I'd found in the guest library downstairs, but my eyes refused to focus. After a minute, I gave up and turned off the bedside lamp. I crawled underneath the sheets and closed my eyes.

I was tiptoeing into the edges of sleep when I felt something move against my bare legs. After the stories of scorpions in the breakfast dishes, I was scared to move. I slowly reached my hand to the light and switched it on. Moving slowly, I peeled the sheets back. My hand shook as I tried not to disturb whatever lay next to me. I held my breath, then I yanked the sheet back and rolled off the bed to land on my back on the floor. I leapt to my feet. On the bed, flicking its tongue was a long, black snake.

Fifteen minutes later, the snake was gone, and my heart rate was back down to normal. I had run screaming down the hallway until Deputy McCall had charged up the stairs with his gun drawn.

"It's just a king snake," Deputy McCall had said. "It probably got in here on a maid's cart or something. It's perfectly harmless. They keep mice away."

Personally, I thought the purpose of the snake was to keep guests away, but I kept this thought to myself. I had a feeling Deputy McCall already considered me a flighty tourist who came to commune with the vortex. Steve and Harmony had offered to let me change rooms, but I reassured them I was fine.

After everyone had left and my door was shut and locked, I combed through the rest of my belongings. I searched slowly and methodically through my suitcase and around my bed. I wanted to make sure that no other creepy crawly thing was hiding out amongst my belongings. I even checked behind my shower curtain. Nothing else appeared to be tampered with and no other desert dweller was in the room.

Exhausted, I crawled back into bed and turned off the light. Despite the long plane ride and excitement of the day, I couldn't fall asleep. Was Brad Cassidy's death linked to the series of mishaps at the spa? Who disliked Steve and Harmony enough to want their business to fail? Was it the realtor in a vain attempt to make the value of their business plummet and force them to sell? What started out as a fun vacation had quickly turned into the vacation from hell. Perhaps Juliet and I should hop on the next plane back to Burlington and head home. All these thoughts swirled around in my head like a pea in a blender until I finally settled into a restless sleep.

The next morning I looked for some toothpicks in my belongings to hold my eyelids open. I had spent the night dreaming about snakes and scorpions in my bed.

"You look like crap," Juliet commented when I entered the dining room for breakfast.

"Thanks," I muttered. "Snakes tend to do that to me."

"Snakes?"

"Someone stuck a snake in my bed last night.

Imagine my surprise when I felt something wiggling next to my leg. I can't believe you didn't hear me screeching."

"I had my earplugs in last night and listened to some meditation music. It helps me focus my energy."

I scooped some scrambled eggs onto my plate. Although bacon wasn't on the menu, the chef made some concessions to the non-vegan guests. At least, I assumed the yellow concoction was eggs. For all I knew, it may have been scrambled tofu. I put some fruit onto my plate as well. At least if Juliet did win the fight and get an all-nude wedding, I would be thin after this trip.

I shuffled my way slowly to a nearby table. Lu sat hovered over a cup of coffee inhaling its scent. When I sat down, she slid the carafe towards me.

"Long night?"

"Yep."

"Any progress?"

"Nope."

"Do we have any suspects?"

"Nope."

Clearly, Lu was not going to give me any information easily. She wasn't a morning person, so I planned to leave her alone until the coffee had worked its magic.

Juliet had other plans. She bounced her way over to the table with a bowl of oatmeal and a cup of tea. She sported a pair of turquoise leggings which showed off her long, thin legs and a white t-shirt. She was barefoot.

"Shoes are a wonderful thing," I said. "They keep snakes and scorpions away from your feet."

She shooed my concerns away with her hand. "I'm going to go do yoga out on the patio after breakfast. Hari K'nai is here at the resort!"

"Hairy quinoa? I don't think I've ever eaten that before, and I don't know that I want to."

"No, Flea. Hari is a famous yogi. She's sitting outside meditating right now!"

"I can barely contain my excitement." I forked a spoonful of eggs into my mouth. They were actually eggs, thank my lucky stars. "Do you think we should head home after last night?"

"No!"

"Please don't," Willow said. She sat down next to me with a cup of greenish brown liquid in a teacup. "I already told my parents you would stay and help us figure out what is going on around here."

Lu chose that moment to wake up and fixed the three of us in her steely gaze. "I don't know how many times I've said it, but law enforcement isn't for amateurs. Even I'm keeping my nose out of this one. Sheriff Martinez has it under control, and she won't appreciate tourists poking around in her investigation."

"It's my parents and I have to look out for them," Willow argued. "I'm just asking Phee and Juls to ask around about the mishaps, not the murder. After all, the deputies don't consider the two matters related. No harm in that, is there?"

"I suppose not, but don't come crying to me when another arm falls off a body."

Looking across the table at Willow's hopeful expression, I knew I couldn't abandon my friend. It was time to go investigate.

CHAPTER SEVEN

Juliet dragged me out to the patio to participate in the morning yoga session. Although not as clumsy as I used to be, downward-facing dog still gave me problems. Juliet could barely contain her heroine worship as she skipped over to introduce herself to Hari.

"I'm Juliet, and this is my sister, Phee," Juliet gushed. Her hands fluttered out towards Hari to shake her hand but dropped it away when the older woman clasped her hands together and gave a slight bow.

"A pleasure to meet you, Juliet. You and your sister are practitioners of yoga?"

"I am. I teach yoga back home in our small town."

"I would definitely say I practice. Maybe if I do it enough times, I might be able to get through one of Juliet's classes without falling over," I joked.

Hari turned her pale gray eyes in my direction. The intensity of her gaze gutted my insides and left me chilled to the bone. Rather than the fuzzy feeling that infused my body after participating in Juliet's yoga classes, no warmth emanated from this woman.

Fortunately, Juliet broke the silence. "I read your book *Pathway to Patience and Peace* five times. You are my heroine."

"Why?"

Juliet shook her head. "What do you mean? I use your book to channel my yogic spirit before teaching my classes. You inspire me to inspire my students."

"How nice," Hari said. "Oh, good. There's Steven." Hari strode across the patio to where Steven stood in his gray shorts and ironed white t-shirt. His socks were so eye-blinding white that I pulled my sunglasses from my head and slipped them on. I watched Hari embrace Steve, her pale hair glinting in the sun and noticed her icy personality thaw as she chatted with him about the upcoming yoga class.

"Dad thinks she's the greatest thing since Woodstock," Willow whispered. "Frankly, I prefer Juliet's teaching to Hari's but don't tell him."

"I won't," I whispered back. "I think I'll pass on the yoga class. I'm going to visit the museum in town."

"Take one of the spa's Jeeps. Mom can get you keys. I'm going to stick close today. The sheriff said they are going to question the staff that weren't here yesterday. Dad's in charge of keeping the guests happy while Mom handles the nitty gritty of Brad's murder."

"Doesn't seem very balanced."

"Mom's the rock. She fits in well here."

I looked around the patio at the guests sitting in lotus position on yoga mats with Steve smack dab in the midst of them with his eyes closed and a beatific smile on his face. Harmony may look the part of a hippie, but Steve was a card-carrying member of the Birkenstock-wearing vortex tribe.

I got the keys to one of the Jeeps from Harmony and headed to Sedona. I did plan to head to the museum, but first I planned to do a little real estate shopping.

Ten minutes later, I pulled up in front of Sun Vortex Realty. The receptionist was on the telephone when I walked in, but she held up a finger to indicate I should wait. I wandered around the front area and picked up a couple of brochures on available property.

"Can I help you?" the receptionist asked.

"Is Francine Whitaker here? I wanted to talk to her about some commercial investment property."

"She's out of the office with a client right now, but Toni Elliot is here. She may be able to answer some questions and get some more information for you."

I hesitated a moment but decided I may as well see if Toni had any information she could share. "That would be great. Thank you."

She buzzed back to an office and a moment later, a young woman in a bronze-colored sundress which muddied her tan complexion walked out to meet me. "Toni Elliot. Nice to meet you."

"O…Olivia…Sutton," I lied.

"How can I help you, Miss Sutton?"

"I'm interested in buying land. Lots of land. As an investment, I mean."

"Okay," Toni said slowly. "Come on back to my office. Let's talk."

I followed her to a small office tastefully decorated in southwestern colors of clay and turquoise. "I'm going to need a little bit more information. What do you plan to do with the land?" Toni asked.

"Well," I lowered my voice and looked around, "my dad owns a string of salons and spas back east, and he sent me out here to scout out possible sites for a westward expansion."

"Really?" I could practically see Toni's ears pricking up in excitement. "I go to New York and Boston quite a bit to visit family. Perhaps I've heard of the salon."

"They are in Vermont," I said quickly. "Tulips Salon and Spa. We have several locations, but Daddy says its time I branch out on my own." I flipped my hair back like I'd seen Juliet do a million times.

"This is a great area for spas. We have a healthy tourism industry here in Sedona and they all have money." Toni blushed and in a flustered voice continued. "I mean, there is definitely a healthy economy to support a new spa."

"I've been looking at some of the existing spas in the area. Just to check out the competition. There's one place that is exactly the type of spa and resort I'm looking to open. I think it was called Harmony Healing or Harmonious Waters…"

"Harmonious Healing?"

I snapped my fingers. "Yes! That's it. I worry that even with the tourism base here, it wouldn't be enough for two very similar locations."

Toni stood up and closed her office door. She sat back down at her desk and leaned conspiratorially towards me. "A little bird told me that Harmonious Healing may be on the market soon. It's not confirmed, so please don't say anything, but for the right price, anything can be bought."

"Is it because business is bad?" I feigned worry over the misspending of my fictitious father's investment dollars.

"No. Well, not really. The owners haven't provided the best level of service possible for their guests, and I've heard they've had many of their guests check out early. I looked at their latest Yelp reviews and business isn't as good as it should be. They built that spa on prime tourist land. Harmony and Steve, the owners, just don't make good business decisions, but you didn't hear that from me." Toni actually winked at me then. If I was at a car lot and she was a used car salesperson, I would have run screaming out of the office. As it was, I was on the case. Clearly, Harmony's suspicions that someone was deliberately sabotaging their business weren't unfounded.

"Hm…sounds like I might be able to get the land for less than the market value is myself," I mused. "Daddy would be thrilled. He keeps a tight hold on my purse strings. It's such a bother sometimes. Can you give me any information at all about the spa? I know it's not for sale yet or anything, but I want to be ready to pounce right on it, if it turns out to be the right fit for our expansion plan."

Toni looked around the office. I looked around, too. Was there someone hiding behind the saguaro cactus listening in? The way she was acting, I was starting to wonder. "I put some information together in anticipation of a possible sale. I overheard my partner Francine saying it may come up for sale. If I give you a copy, you have to keep it strictly hush hush for now. Not even Francine knows I put this brochure together."

"Oh, I will," I promised. "I wouldn't want the competition buying it out from under me."

Toni opened her desk drawer and pulled a glossy folder with a picture of the spa prominently displayed on the front. Her eyes darted around her office again before sliding it across the desk to me. I felt like a drug dealer on a street corner as I hurriedly stuffed the folder into my large purse.

I stood up. My acting skills were waning, and I was ready to leave before the cops came and busted this illicit brochure deal.

"I'll be in touch with you after I talk to Daddy," I promised.

"Do you have a business card? I can send you other potential property information."

I pretended to dig through my purse for one. "Dang it! I switched from my city bag to my vacation bag and left them back at the hotel. I'll call you."

"What hotel are you staying at? I can drop off some more information if you'll be in town for a few days."

I pretended to hear my cell phone and snatched it out of my bag. "Hello?" I wiggled my fingers goodbye and scurried out of the real estate office as fast as my short legs could carry me.

CHAPTER EIGHT

After I drove away from the Sun Vortex Realty, I drove around exploring downtown Sedona. I located the museum and decided to see what I could find out about the sacred sites of the Yavapai tribe. I paid the admission fee and wandered around the museum. Despite its small size, it had an impressive collection of Native American artifacts and exhibits about the history of the area. I eventually found an exhibit that detailed the creation story. There was no reference to a specific site for the birth of the tribe.

I finished my tour and made my way back to the front desk where a bored teenager sat glued to his cell phone.

"Excuse me," I said.

He glanced up briefly from his screen before returning his text conversation. "Yes?"

"Is there anyone here who can tell me about the Yavapai tribe and their history?"

"Mr. Butters can." His fingers continued to fly across his phone. He texted faster with his thumbs than I could type on a computer keyboard.

"Is he here?" I tried to keep the exasperation from my voice. Was I really getting old enough to be annoyed by teenagers already?

"Yep."

"Where can I find him?"

The teen sighed, and with an annoyed expression, he pointed towards the closed door to my left. It had a sign that read "Museum Staff Only."

"Do you need to call him out here or can I just go back?" I swear I wanted to rip the cell phone out of his hands and stomp on it, but I'm sure I would end up in handcuffs if I did. I was still tempted. "Oh! Just never mind."

I stomped my way over to the staff door and yanked it open. An older man with a shiny dome-shaped head looked up startled. I stomped my way to his desk and huffed, "Phee Jefferson and you have the worst customer service person ever sitting out there."

"It's my nephew," the man said.

"Oh. I'm sorry. He just wouldn't stop texting when I wanted to ask about the Yavapai tribe."

He motioned for me to take a seat and rubbed his bald head as if he was patting down a stray hair. "I understand. If he weren't my sister's only child, I would have fired him months ago. I'm Dr. Jerry Butters, by the way. What would you like to know about the Yavapai tribe?

"I wanted to know more about the location of their sacred sites and in particular, the site tied to their creation story."

"That's a difficult question to answer. There are several variations of the story. Creation stories change over time or different clans within the tribe have variations. The primary story is that many years ago the ancestors of the Yavapai, who are the People of the Sun, came up from the underworld on the first corn plant into a big hole called the Montezuma Well."

"Is that an actual place around here?" I asked.

"It is, but it's about thirty miles from Sedona."

"Are there any sacred sites nearby? Any near Harmonious Healing Spa?" I asked. I had decided to cut to the chase. Hanging around with Lu had taught me that sometimes pussyfooting around an issue didn't always get you the information you needed.

"Ah. I see you've been talking to Idelia Riggs." Dr. Butters sat up straight and his friendly smile disappeared from his face. "I've already told her that I won't be dragged into any of her so-called claims. I'm a scientist and I deal with facts, not dreams."

"You misunderstand me. I've never met Idelia Riggs. I'm friends with Harmony and Steve's daughter, Willow. They own Harmonious Healing."

"I know them. Good people. Idelia has been a thorn in their side for months." He looked around and lowered his voice. "Is it true Brad Cassidy was killed there yesterday?"

"How did you hear about it?" I asked. I hadn't looked at the local newspaper this morning to see if there had been a news article on his death.

"My sister is a dispatcher for the sheriff's office. She came home last night after her shift last night all in a tither about it. She and my nephew Franklin live with me right now. She's going through a divorce and well…she's my sister."

"Did you know Brad?"

"Just from running into him at the coffee shop. My sister knew him from some of the social things she's gone to for the newly single."

"Brad was divorced?" I asked.

"Yes. He was married to Marianne who works there at the spa. There was no love lost between the two of them. From what I heard, they were already separated when he got a job at the spa in some last-ditch attempt to reconcile with her. According to the town grapevine, Marianne caught him doing the dastardly deed with a someone there at the spa. He got fired and got served with divorce papers all on the same day," Dr. Butters whispered as he leaned across the desk.

"Really?" I whispered back.

Dr. Butters sat up and straightened his dark green sweater vest. "I don't like to spread gossip."

"I understand. I'm the same way." I stood up to go. "You've been very helpful, Dr. Butters, and such a pleasure to speak with. I hope to see you again before I leave to go back home."

A light tinge of pink suffused his cheeks and traveled to his ears which flushed bright red. "A pleasure indeed, Miss Jefferson. Please tell Steve and Harmony I said hello."

I left the museum without a backward glance at the teenager who was still glued to his phone. I needed caffeine and calories.

I headed down the street looking for a coffee shop. A few blocks west and I spotted a sign reading Common Grounds with a picture of a coffee cup next to it. My version of heaven should have coffee readily available at all times and lots of chocolate that never causes weight gain.

I walked through the front door of the shop and the smell of coffee and baked goods nearly made me swoon. I gave the barista my order of a large latte and a bacon cheddar scone. Minutes later I was situated at a small table overlooking the street. The first bite of the scone just reinforced my decision that I could never be vegan. Bacon made of tofu could never equal the real deal.

I pulled out my telephone and dialed Clint's number. Clint and I had weathered our rocky patch and seemed to be on the path to something more permanent, but I wasn't pushing. He had revealed how difficult his life had been with his parents' constant sniping and his father's death by suicide. These were all things I never knew and no one ever talked about. I understood why he feared marriage, but I wasn't giving up hope.

"Hello beautiful. I was just thinking about you," Clint's said.

"I missed you." I said simply. I did. I missed

his smile and the way it made me feel butterflies every time I saw it. I missed him falling asleep ten minutes into my romantic 1940s movies. Dang his sexy self for making me love him!

"I miss you, too. Your ten-ton cat misses you, but I've been letting him sleep on your pillow."

"Pushover."

"Ferdie's big enough that I think he could take me out with one swipe of his kitty paw," Clint chuckled. "How's the investigation?"

"Investigation?"

"Yes, Ophelia, the investigation. You remember the dead body in the freezer last night, don't you? Are you telling me you aren't curious about who killed him?"

"Maybe a little."

"That's my girl. What have you found out so far?"

"Seriously? No warnings to be careful or lectures about how I'm making you have high blood pressure?"

"Thanks for taking care of saying what I was going to say, but I promised I'd quit being a control freak."

I was skeptical about his change of heart. I decided to test the waters. "Someone stuck a snake in my bed last night."

"Well, clearly it wasn't poisonous or we wouldn't be talking."

Hmm…round one went to Clint. I decided to try to poke the bear a little bit harder. "I went to the real estate office and to the museum and interrogated some suspects."

"How'd that go for you?"

Oh, he was good. Cooler than a penguin in a freezer with a popsicle. "Pretty good. I found out that the spa isn't on sacred ground and the realtor is up to no good. I plan on tracking down the guy I saw arguing with one of the employees right before the murder and follow him."

"Absolutely not!"

"Ha! I knew it! It's killing you that I'm poking into this murder. Lu told you about the snake already, didn't she?"

I heard him sigh and had a vision of him running his fingers through his dark hair. "She did. Asking questions is one thing. Tracking suspects is a whole new ballgame and one I can't help you win a thousand miles away from you."

"I was kidding about tracking the man down. I don't even know who he is. I was trying to make you crack like a nut in a squirrel's mouth. I really did try to stay away from a life of crime. I can't help it if the murders love me."

"You're killing me."

"I know. I promise to have Lu with me if I try to tackle any killers."

"Okay. I need to go, Phee. I have to go on patrol. Someone needs to pay for that weekly fifty-pound bag of cat food that panther you own eats."

"He's not fat. He's big-boned," I protested.

"Love you and your big-boned cat. Stay safe and call me tonight."

"Love you, too," I said softly. "Bye."

After tossing my cell phone back into my purse, I leaned back and spent the next few minutes enjoying my coffee and scone and imagining Clint in his blue jeans. All too soon, it was time for me to head back to the spa and its bacon-free zone. Thank goodness, I had a murder to distract me.

CHAPTER NINE

"Where did you disappear to?" Juliet gave me an accusatory look as she plopped down in the chair next to me.

"I went in search of meat. I hunted it down and ate it. It was tasty." I said. I had snuck back into the resort and changed into my bathing suit so I could enjoy my book next to the pool.

"Nice. While you were off gallivanting after food, I sweated my rear off during yoga with Hari and poked around for some more information on our guy Brad. Marianne isn't here today, but not because she's mourning her ex-husband. They were already separated when he got a job here. She wasn't too happy that Harmony hired him, but she stayed here and tried to make the best of it. She and Brad's divorce proceedings put some of these Hollywood breakups to shame. They didn't have much, but Brad wanted every bit of it according to Rose, the girl who was cleaning my room. Turns out, Marianne had a nest egg of cash left to her by her grandmother when she died. She was saving it to open up her own spa one day, but Brad was trying to get half of it in the divorce."

"Sounds like she had a reason to be happy he was gone. So, who was the guy I saw her arguing with yesterday then?"

"New boyfriend? I don't know. Rose likes to gossip and seemed to know the dirt on everyone in this place."

Marianne and Brad were not friendly exes. Although that gave her a reason to kill him, Brad looked like a big guy and Marianne was petite. Would he turn his back on his ex-wife if they had such an acrimonious relationship?

"We need to know when he died," I said.

"Why?"

"Because Marianne was giving you a spa treatment yesterday afternoon, and then right after that she was arguing with the guy on the patio. She has an alibi for at least an hour or so yesterday. We need to know her schedule for yesterday."

"How did she get Brad in the freezer? She definitely couldn't have carried him in there."

"Mr. Manbun could have helped her."

"Who is Mr. Manbun?" Juliet asked.

"The man she was arguing with had a man bun. We don't know his name so for now he is Mr. Manbun." I leaned back against the headrest of the lounger. "I don't want to think about murder right now. We're on vacation. I would like to enjoy at least an hour of peaceful reading by the pool without a murder." I closed my eyes and let the sun warm me.

"Then you don't get this." Juliet snatched my paperback from where it rested on my lap.

"Hey! Give me that back!" I protested.

"It's a murder mystery which means there is murder. It is off today's list of reading choices."

I stuck my tongue out at her and grabbed my book. "It doesn't count because it's fiction, not nonfiction. Besides, I find murder mysteries relaxing."

"You can thank me later."

"For what?"

"I brought you out here for a girls' vacation. I wanted fun in the sun and you wanted a week's relaxation. You said it yourself, murder mysteries are relaxing. I've fulfilled my mission." Juliet smirked at me.

"Hardy har har. You're a regular recreation director, aren't you? Now go away so I can get some more freckles and read the end of this mystery. I'll see you at lunch. Rumor has it that we are getting tofurkey Caesar salads."

"Yummers." Juliet left and went back inside the resort.

I picked up my mystery and tried to read. I love the Chee and Leaphorn mysteries by Tony Hillerman, but the murder in the red rocks on the Navajo reservation were not holding my attention as much as the murder in the freezer here. I sighed and pulled on my cover-up. Dang Juliet and her "murder is relaxing" spiel. At this rate, I would need a vacation in Antarctica if I ever wanted a chance to read a book uninterrupted by murder.

I changed out of my bathing suit and into capris, a turquoise sleeveless top and tennis shoes. My fear of snakes and scorpions had killed any desire I had to wear cute, open-toed shoes for this vacation. I twisted my long hair back into a French twist and headed downstairs to ferret out any information I could about the investigation.

As luck would have it, Lu was coming out of her room as I was leaving mine. Surely, she wasn't going to sit idly by and let the he-man deputies make her look bad.

"What's shakin', bacon?" I greeted her.

"Is that a cop joke?" Lu scowled at me.

"Oops! Definitely not. I had a bacon and cheddar scone in town, so I have bacon on my mind. Sorry."

"And you didn't think to bring me one? Real women eat meat. I love animals as much as the next girl, but I can't stand tofu. I could go vegetarian if I didn't have to eat that squishy, wiggly white blech." Lu stuck her finger in her mouth and pretended to gag.

I gave Lu an apologetic look. "It was a side trip after I went to find out about the real estate agent who is trying to push Steve and Harmony to sell the spa. Turns out that the agency already has a beautiful brochure ready for any potential buyers. I guess Francine is confident that Harmonious Healing's business is on a downward slide that will force them to sell."

"Interesting. It gives credence to the theory that she's behind all of the bad stuff happening to the guests, but do you think someone is going to commit murder for a sale?" Lu asked. "Of course,

I've seen someone killed over a sandwich when I was on patrol in New York, so I guess anything is possible."

I dug around in my straw bag I had purchased for this vacation and pulled out the slick brochures from the realtor. Lu perused them for a minute then handed them back. "Have you heard anything else about the investigation?"

"Nah. The locals aren't going to go out of their way to keep me in the loop. Right now, Deputy McCann is in the employee's lounge questioning staff. He's been holed up in there all morning."

"Poor Harmony and Steve. This investigation is going to hurt their business even more than the pranks. Nobody wants to be interrogated when they are trying to relax and enjoy their vacation."

Lu and I looked around for Willow, but after a few minutes and a call to her room with no result, we assumed she was with her parents. I called Juliet's room from the house phone and asked her if she wanted to go visit the vortex with Lu and me. After my ear recovered from her glass-shattering squeal of joy, I told her we'd see her downstairs in five minutes. Two minutes later she was down the stairs and out the door urging us to hurry up before we missed all the fun.

Lu took the keys to the Jeep from me, and we headed out to experience the healing power of the vortex. Fifteen minutes later, we pulled up to the site listed in Juliet's guidebook.

A round-faced, older woman greeted us at the entrance gate of Crescent Moon Park. "Good afternoon. Welcome fellow traveler on this spiritual path to a more fulfilling life."

"I am so excited!" Juliet bounced up and down in the back seat of the Jeep. "I hope this journey will give me powerful blessing vibes for my wedding."

"The vortex is exciting and growth inspiring. I'm sure the energy will wash over you and help you have greater clarity and insight into your life and your relationship with others," the woman said. She took our entrance fee and gave us a brochure with information and directions to the vortex from the park entrance.

"This is the Cathedral Rock Vortex," Juliet explained, as she read the brochure. "It's supposed to help emphasize your feminine nature."

"Great," Lu said dryly. "Maybe I will start wearing heels on the job. Clint would love having a partner who toddled down the street after a criminal rather than a full-on run. Miller's Cove itself may not have too much crime, but some of the more remote areas of the county are starting to have some problems. Drug manufacturing is taking over rural areas."

"Ugh!" Juliet protested. "Keep your negative news and vibes away from me. You might mess up my wedding blessing I'm going to ask the spirits for while I'm here."

Lu rolled her eyes and shot me an amused look. "Are you sure she's your sister?"

"I ask myself that every day." I laughed.

"The guide says after we park, we have to hike up a creek bed to Cathedral Rock. That's where the vortex is." Juliet read from the brochure, clearly ignoring Lu and me.

"I knew we'd end up hiking on this vacation. Come with me to a spa, she said. It will be relaxing, she said. I can't believe I fell for that sales pitch," I grumbled, but I gave Juliet an affectionate look.

"Walking daily is an excellent form of exercise. I'm just looking out for your health," Juliet replied.

Lu pulled up to a parking spot where several other vehicles were. We all climbed out of the Jeep. Juliet slung a water bottle holder over her shoulder and we headed off towards our cosmic destiny.

Twenty minutes later we and a group of folks we had met on the trail arrived at the vortex. I was surprised to see so many people standing in the area. Not all were standing. Some were sitting cross-legged with their eyes closed. Juliet was in her element. Her bouncy exuberance from earlier had morphed into a calmness I usually saw from her during her yoga classes.

Lu and I left her communing with the energy and wandered around to people watch. There was a wide array of folks present. I saw aging hippies, young people in high-end hiking gear, and grandmas that would look more at home with a cup of tea and knitting needles.

"Do you feel anything?" I asked Lu.

"No. You?"

I stopped and closed my eyes to see if I could feel any kind of weird energy. I did feel a little bit dizzy but that may have been due to the sun and the hike.

"Maybe. I'm not sure. I don't feel like I'm going to start speaking to Willow's spirit guides any time soon."

"Thank goodness. She and Juliet are bad enough. I'm banking on you to keep it at an even balance of rational versus woo woo."

I laughed and that caused a few nearby energy worshipers to give me the evil eye. I suppressed a giggle and motioned Lu to follow me to a nearby rock under a scraggly looking desert tree. Even with my sun hat protecting my fair complexion, I could feel my freckles darkening by the second.

We sat there talking about happenings back in Miller's Cove and let Juliet enjoy her mind meld with the vortex. After about fifteen minutes, we stood up and wandered back over to her.

"We'd better head back to the resort, Juls. My freckles can't take much more baking in the sun."

"I'm ready." Juliet gave me a beatific smile. "Wade and I are going to have the best marriage."

"I could have told you that and we didn't have

to travel a thousand miles for that bit of wisdom."

Juliet sighed and shook her head. "One day, you'll realize there is more to this world than you can see with your eyes."

We hiked back to the parking lot and headed back towards town. Juliet sat in the backseat with a glazed smile on her face. Lu and I tried to keep a straight face as we headed back towards the spa.

As we turned onto the road that led to Harmonious Healing, the Jeep began to sputter and lurch. A moment later, it gave a last hiccupping jerk and died. Lu quickly shifted into neutral and steered the Jeep to the side of the road.

"Dang it! What the heck is wrong with this thing?" Lu said. She attempted to start it, but it only sputtered and died again.

"Is it out of gas?" I asked.

"No way. It had over a half a tank when we left the vortex. I always check fuel level in vehicles. It's a cop thing. We don't want to be in mid-chase and have to pull over to fill the tank up."

I pulled out my phone to call the resort. Willow could come pick us up. "No signal."

"My phone doesn't have a signal either," Juliet said.

"I guess we walk," Lu said. She pulled the keys out of the ignition and climbed out of the Jeep. She slammed the door.

I sighed and pulled the sunscreen out of my bag. I slathered my bare arms, legs and face with SPF100 lotion and prayed for a sudden cloud cover. Once I was guaranteed not to burn for at least thirty minutes, I got out of the car and stood next to Lu and Juliet.

"Here's your happy thought for the day. It's only two miles to the resort, and someone is bound to pass us and give us a ride the rest of the way up there." Juliet's attempt to cheer us was met with two sets of raised eyebrows and skeptical snorts.

We trudged our way through the dry heat towards the resort. Ten dusty minutes later, no car had passed and the heat rising in a life draining wave from the asphalt had driven us to the dusty side of the road. I thanked my lucky stars that I had worn tennis shoes. My scorpion fear had paid off in the long run.

"I plan to take a long shower set at icemaker temperature and then I plan to drink a gallon of lemonade followed by a mojito," Juliet said.

"I second that sentiment, but it may be a gallon of mojitos followed by a lemonade," Lu joked.

"I plan on the shower, the mojito and a margarita followed by another shower. I'm planning our next girls' getaway. I've heard Siberia is nice this time of year." I pulled off my hat and used it to fan my face for a minute before plopping it back on my head.

After a thirty-minute walk, we stumbled into the resort. Willow was sitting in the guest lounge chatting with the geologist when we made our dusty entrance.

"What in the spirits' names happened to you three?" she asked.

I held up a finger to her. I poured three large glasses of water from the pitcher set out for guests on the sideboard, passed two glasses to Juliet and Lu before downing mine. After I refilled and drank a second glass, I turned to answer Willow.

"The Jeep broke down."

"What? How is that possible? It's only six months old," Willow protested.

"Tell it that," Juliet said from the chair where she sprawled in a sweaty but pretty heap sipping her water.

"I'll let Mom know and she'll have Miguel tow it to the mechanic. You should have called me. I would have picked you up."

I gave her a look that would have made a woman made of a weaker personality cry. "No cell service."

"I am so sorry. I can't believe the spirits didn't warn me that you were in trouble," Willow said.

"Maybe they didn't have cell service either," Lu said. At Willow's hurt look, she added, "Well, I don't know how they send their messages. Analog? Digital? It's all a mystery to me."

I couldn't help but laugh, and the tension was

broken. It wasn't Willow's fault the Jeep had died. I'm sure the spirits' skills didn't include mechanical repairs. I had sweated off at least five pounds and planned to reward myself with an extra helping of black bean burger at dinner.

"I'm heading to my room to shower and take a short nap before dinner." I gave Willow a quick hug to let her know I knew it wasn't her fault and headed to my room.

Two hours later, I sat down in the dining room with everyone. I felt refreshed and rested although my skin was tinged pink despite my sunscreen. Steve's demeanor had gone from peaceful to pinched and Harmony was nervously twisting her ring. The dining room was full of guests though, so maybe news of the murder hadn't reached tourists' ears. Either that or murder groupies had descended upon the resort.

"Marianne's been taken into custody," Willow said quietly as I sat down.

"What? When? She murdered Brad?"

"Sheriff Martinez asked her to come down to the sheriff's office, but everyone else has been interviewed here at the resort. They had talked to her last night when they found the body. This afternoon the deputies completed their interviews and left. Two hours later, Sheriff Martinez showed up here and took Marianne in the cruiser to the station," Harmony explained.

"She didn't kill Brad," Steve said vehemently. "She's got such a positive aura. No one with that kind of soul could take another person's life."

"It will be okay, Dad," Willow reached over and hugged Steve.

"No, it won't," he said. He pulled off his glasses and pinched the bridge of his nose. He took a deep breath and when he looked at us, tears glistened in his eyes. "Harmony and I've worked so hard to make this a place of healing and love. All our work and energy has been for nothing. Someone has darkened the heart of this place and I don't know that I can fix it."

"I'm not giving this place up without a fight," Harmony said fiercely. "I don't believe Marianne killed Brad either. I still think it has something to do with all the other crap that's taken place. Mark my words, when this is all said or done, it's about this business, not a bad divorce turned ugly."

CHAPTER TEN

Dinner was a subdued affair after that as we settled down to our bean burgers and our own thoughts. The dining room was filled with conversations and laughter from the other diners in sharp contrast to our own silence.

I decided to share what I'd learned earlier that day during my trip into Sedona. I hoped it would make Harmony and Steve feel better. "I stopped by the museum today and talked to Dr. Butters. He says that from what he knows, this place is not built on sacred ground and that Idelia Riggs is full of beans. He didn't use those exact words, but that's the gist of the conversation."

"That's good news!" Willow said and gave her parents a hopeful look. "Maybe we should confront Idelia with the facts."

"It won't do any good. People believe what they want to believe. So far, we've done a good job on keeping Idelia's story that we built this place on a sacred site quiet, but I don't want to poke the hornet's nest by going toe-to-toe with her. Not right now anyway," Harmony said. She poked at her dinner with her fork. She sighed and finally gave up on her food. "We should have stayed in California."

"Don't say that, Honey Bear! We can't give up yet. I know things are tough right now, but we are doing good here. People's energies are healing. Their spirits come back refreshed and renewed.

All this will blow over and we'll be back on track to creating a beautiful retreat full of love and good vibes."

I didn't believe in Steve's New Age spiel, but I did think that Harmonious Healing was a great place and deserved to have a chance to succeed without all this chaos and negative publicity.

"Did the deputies tell you anything more about the investigation?" I asked.

Willow put down her fork and lowered her voice. "Brad definitely died by the obvious knife in the back. That dude had some bad juju going on though. Not only did he and Marianne have a bad relationship over money, he had a bad relationship with the Navajo Nation and his gambling debt at their casino."

"I bet that was why he was so hot to get ahold of Marianne's inheritance. He probably owed people money. Maybe they did just take Marianne down to talk to her and get an official statement," Juliet said.

I thought about it. "If he owed money over gambling, it might pay to poke and find out who was supporting his gambling habit since Marianne cut off his funds."

"I don't mean to rain on anyone's karmic parade, but Marianne is a viable suspect," Lu said. "She was here at the spa yesterday at the time he was murdered. She had motive. This case is almost a slam dunk."

"But, Lu," I protested. "How did he get into

the freezer? She's too small to drag him. She would have had to convince him to go into the freezer with her and if they were at odds, this doesn't add up in my mind."

"I want to know why none of the kitchen staff found him before then," Juliet said.

"That is one question I can answer," Harmony said. "The kitchen staff pull out all their prep for dinner right before they take their break. The chef always has a fifteen-minute break for all the staff where they can taste new desserts she's working on or a new dish right before prep for dinner starts. None of them would have had a reason to go back into the freezer until the next day."

"That means Brad was murdered in that fifteen-minute window," I said. Interesting. That narrowed down the list of suspects substantially. It had to be someone who knew the ins and outs of the kitchen staff which means it had to be a current or former employee. It was looking worse rather than better for Marianne.

"So how come the waitress went into the freezer," Juliet asked.

"The chef has a bad knee and kept her ice wraps in the freezer for when the swelling gets too bad. She sent the waitress in there to grab one during the dinner rush because she couldn't leave the line herself," Steve answered.

"Convenient, if you ask me." Juliet narrowed her eyes in suspicion. "What do we know about this chef character?"

"Kathy? We were lucky to get her. She's an up and coming young chef. She wouldn't have given someone like Brad the time of day," Harmony said. She pushed her full plate away. A waitress rushed up to remove it. When she asked if she could bring Harmony some dessert, Harmony shook her head no and asked for a cup of herbal tea instead.

"Women have hooked up with men who no one else would believe is a good match," I said.

"Exactly. Look at Wade and me. I love peace and yoga. He's an ex-Marine. Total opposites. No one in a million years would have predicted we would work, but we do."

"Juliet's right," Lu chimed in. "We don't know what goes on in people's hearts and personal lives. Stranger things have happened."

"Maybe," Steve nodded his head, "but they haven't found a connection between Brad and anyone else yet. Marianne was his connection with Sedona."

"Where are they from?" I asked.

"Oregon, if I recall correctly. Or maybe it was Washington. Or maybe it was Oklahoma. I don't remember." Steve shook his head as if hoping the answer would fall out and land on the table in front of him.

"Enough of this negative energy at the dinner table. I would like to propose that after we eat, we head to our living quarters and I host a reading with the stones to try to figure out what is going on," Willow announced.

I stifled a groan. I was tired even after my afternoon nap, but one look at Willow's eager face and I knew I would go. Lu raised her eyebrow in a question to me. I nodded and she said she planned to go and asked who else was in. After we had all agreed to Willow's plan, the rest of dinner passed quickly.

Willow asked us to give her a few minutes to get her stones ready. Juliet, Lu and I decided to sit outside with a glass of wine until our spirit session. The sun was setting and the beauty of the desert surrounded us. Although it wasn't the lush green of the eastern part of the country that I was used to, the red rocks and stark landscape possessed its own beauty. I could see why Steve and Harmony loved it here.

A sudden scuffing sound around the corner of the building startled us out of our quiet contemplation of the day. Lu shot up out of her seat and handed Juliet her wine glass. She moved like a panther stalking a rabbit around the corner of the building. A second later, we heard a startled yell and Lu's sharp command to stop.

Juliet and I put down our glasses and ran after Lu. She didn't need us though. When we came around the corner, she had Mr. Manbun down on the ground in a move that would have made Pepper Anderson proud.

"It's Mr. Manbun!" I exclaimed.

"Let me up!"

"Not until you tell me what you were doing skulking around looking in windows," Lu growled. She tightened her hold on his arm. "Phee, call the police."

"No! Wait!" Mr. Manbun said. "I was looking for Marianne. She was supposed to meet me after she got off her shift today, but she never showed. Can you let me up now?"

Lu eased off him. He rolled over and sat up. His hand lifted to smooth his hair which had retained its tightly coiled bun during the scuffle.

"Who are you and how do you know Marianne?" I demanded.

"Luke Jackson and Marianne's my girlfriend. At least I hope she still is after our argument last night."

"Marianne is talking to the sheriff right now. Where were you yesterday?" Juliet glared at him with her best steely-eyed seventies girl cop gaze.

"Me? I was at work." He stood up and brushed himself off.

"Really? Then how come I saw you arguing with Marianne on the patio yesterday afternoon?" I asked.

Lu grabbed his arm again. "I think we should call the sheriff and let Deputy McCall question him."

"Wait! I was at work yesterday. Listen. I admit I was here yesterday for five minutes maybe ten. I work two jobs. Once I finished my shift at the auto body shop where I work, I headed to my second job as a bartender at a local restaurant here in Sedona called the Blue Cactus. I ran up here to see Marianne in between shifts. She gave me a hard time about blowing off our plans for the evening to cover a shift for my buddy, Ray, at the restaurant. She doesn't understand why I've been working so much lately. It was a normal fight. No big deal."

"Why are you working so much? Do you have a gambling problem?" Juliet eyed him suspiciously.

"What? Me? No way. That was her ex, Brad. I'm working to save up for something important. Wait a minute. Did you say that Marianne was at the sheriff's office? Did I mishear you?"

"You heard it right. Marianne's a suspect in her ex-husband's murder. He was found dead here at the resort last night."

"What?" Luke sagged and leaned against the wall. "And they think Marianne killed him? No way. Marianne hated his guts, but they were over. She didn't have a reason to kill him."

"What about him wanting part of her inheritance from her grandmother?" I asked. "That could have driven her to the point she wanted to kill him."

"No. Not possible." Luke shook his head. "Marianne's attorney reassured her that there was no way that the inheritance was subject to the divorce settlement. Besides, it was pretty much wrapped up. He couldn't afford his attorney's fees and had agreed to sign off on it all. Brad had told Marianne that he was done gambling."

"Interesting," Juliet nodded her head like she was a wise man on top of the mountain. "It takes away one motive to kill him, but is Marianne hated him so much, Brad could have pissed her off so bad that she snapped."

"I doubt it. If she was going to snap, it would have been one of the many times she caught him cheating. She hated him, but they were over. She didn't have a reason to kill him. Can I go now? I need to get to Marianne. I've got to make sure she's okay."

Lu released him again. "You can go, but I'll be sure to tell Sheriff Martinez you were here. Don't leave town."

Luke shook his head, a hint of fear in his eye at Lu's harsh warning. She could be intimidating if she needed to be. He took off and we headed back to our glasses of wine.

"Do you believe him?" I asked Lu.

"No reason not to believe him yet. Like I said, Marianne's the most likely suspect, but that doesn't mean she's the only one. This case is turning out to be more interesting than I thought it would be."

"I'm glad you're entertained by this vacation fiasco," I said. "The spirits better make it up to me. That's all I'm saying."

CHAPTER ELEVEN

We joined Willow, Steve and Harmony in their living room. Willow had dragged a coffee table into the middle of the room and surrounded it with cushions. She motioned for us to sit down. I groaned as I tried cross my legs. My thighs didn't love me from all the hiking today. I promised myself I would join the yoga class in the morning to stretch out my tight muscles.

"If we could all join hands, it will help the spirits communicate better."

Juliet grabbed my hand. I hesitated before grabbing Lu's because she didn't strike me as the hand-holding type of girl although she and Anthony had been doing quite a bit of it from what I heard from the sheriff's office grapevine also known as Clint.

Feeling brave, I snatched her hand and was rewarded with a look that would freeze a rabbit in its place. She really was good with the looks. She was going to make a great mom one day. Anthony was a lucky man and a brave one.

Willow wasn't intimidated by Lu. She reached over and grabbed Lu's hand with a peaceful smile which brooked no argument from Lu. After we were all in a circle, Willow instructed us to close our eyes and sit in silence while she attempted to contact her spirit guides.

I closed my eyes and tried to empty my brain of any interfering thoughts. I'd tried meditation after Juliet promised it would give me greater focus. I still couldn't sit still or quiet my mind for more than a minute at a time. Either Juliet had greater self-control than I did, or she had less stuff in her brain to empty. As her older sister, I voted for the latter.

"They're here," Willow said. "They are speaking to me."

I felt rather than heard Lu's derisive snort. She had a better poker face than I did. It was a good thing the lights were dim and our eyes were closed.

"The spirits are worried," Willow intoned. "They see great danger here, and they are clamoring for us to stop it."

"What kind of danger?" Juliet asked, fear tinging her usually confident voice.

I opened one eye and glanced at my sister. Worry wrinkled her usually serene face. The spirits better not be feeding us a line of baloney or they would have to deal with me.

"The spirits say we shouldn't assume we know all ties. There are ties that are temporary and ties that are permanent. They say once we know the ties that are permanent, we will be able to find the answer."

"Ties? What do they mean by ties?" Steve asked.

I wondered why Steve wasn't talking to the spirits himself. Isn't that where Steve went for answers. I wondered what Harmony thought about her husband and daughter's relationship with the spirit world. Was she a believer? I would love to have Harmony by herself and ask her more about it, but now was not the time.

"The spirits just keep repeating find the ties, Daddy. You know their messages can be jumbled."

Lu didn't suppress her snort this time and the spell was broken. We all opened our eyes and blinked in the light. I looked around at everyone. Juliet looked frightened. Steve's and Harmony's faces were both pinched with fatigue and worry. Lu just looked bored.

Willow gave Lu an appraising gaze. "You doubt me, but the spirits tell me that you will have a new family tie in your life soon, too."

"I don't think Anthony and I are ready for marriage yet. We're both too busy with our jobs right now," Lu said.

"Hmm…" Willow smiled and turned to her parents. "I think we need to pull the employees' files."

"What? Why?" Steve asked.

"We need to see who the next of kin are for all of the people that work for you," Juliet chimed in. She knew what Willow was looking for and so did I. We needed to know if there were any relatives that we didn't know of that had access to the resort.

"These people are our family," Steve protested.

"Steve, we need to do this. Brad was one of our employees, too. Clearly, he wasn't of a family mindset. We need to do this," Harmony said, laying her hand on his. "I'll look through all of them to see what I can find. I can't let you girls see them. Employee privacy is important."

"I don't like it," Steve said, "but I guess it needs to be done."

"I can't believe you guys are taking these so-called spirit guides seriously," Lu said. "I mean, sure, we should look through employees' files, but do you really think the spirits can solve this crime? Good old every day detective work is what is going to solve this, not ghosts."

"The spirits are not ghosts," Willow said. "They are more than that. I think of them as angels trying to help humanity."

"Well, my priest might take umbrage with that idea," Lu said, "but okay."

"We are all one on this plane of existence, Lu. None of us knows what happens after this, but some of us are open to communicate with other realms," Willow said in her wise woman voice.

"I don't necessarily believe in all this New Age stuff, but I think your spirit guides, or whatever they are, are spot on with looking at people's backgrounds. That's just good solid police work and if this was my case, it's what I would do," Lu said. She stood up. "It's been a long night and I'm ready for some shut-eye. I'll see you guys in the morning."

Juliet and I got up to leave, too. It had been a long day between the hike to the vortex and the long, dusty walk back to the resort. I had a phone date with Clint, too.

Juliet took pity on me and helped me search my room for any critters that might want to snuggle up with me tonight. My room was snake and scorpion free, so I was guaranteed a good night's sleep. I climbed into my cartoon coyote pajamas that I'd purchased just for this trip. I wish I had remembered to pack my skunk slippers. My feet felt naked without them.

I picked up my phone and dialed Clint's number. He answered after several rings.

"Did I wake you?" I asked.

"Yes, but I don't mind." He yawned and it struck me that I had forgotten about the time difference.

"I'm sorry, sweetheart. I forgot how late it is there."

"I'd rather hear your voice than sleep, but even when you're not here in bed next to me, I dream about you."

I felt a tingle in my toes at his sexy, sleep-filled voice. I wished I was back home curled under the covers with Clint. "I miss you. I can't wait to see your face and cuddle up next to you."

"When you get home, I plan to do more than just cuddle with you," Clint said in a husky voice. "I love you, woman. Hurry up and get home to me."

"I love you, too. Go back to sleep and I'll call you in the morning."

"Okay. Good night, love."

I disconnected and let the warm feeling that I always felt with him push out the negative experiences of the day. I settled into bed and was asleep before I could count the second sheep.

CHAPTER TWELVE

I awoke from a deep sleep. I had been dreaming I was at Juliet's wedding and everyone was naked, but I was dressed in a snowsuit with pink bunny slippers on my feet. The stuff of nightmares except for the bunny slippers. I was putting those on my shopping list. I glanced at my phone to see what time it was. Three o'clock in the morning. Practically the witching hour or was that three twenty? My stomach growled in protest at the early hour.

I got out of bed and pulled on a robe. I was starving. Hopefully, they had something stashed in the kitchen that I could fix without making a mess. I'd be happy with a peanut butter and jelly sandwich.

I tiptoed my way down to the kitchen. As I opened the swinging doors, I had to cover my eyes to the blinding glare of the overhead lights. Willow and Juliet looked up from where they stood hunched over their plates eating sandwiches.

"Fwee? Mwaht are fwoo doing hewah?" Juliet mumbled through mouthful of sandwich. She swallowed and took a gulp of mile. "Sorry. What are you doing up?"

"I'm starving. Feed me or I'll start gnawing on my straw purse."

Willow handed me a jar of peanut butter with a knife still stuck in it. Juliet slid a jar of homemade pear cactus jelly next to the load of thick, fresh bread the two of them had hacked several slices from.

"Give up the rest," I demanded.

"What?" Juliet said with a guilty look at Willow. "I have known you your entire life. Hand over the potato chips and no one has to get hurt."

Juliet sighed and reached under the counter and into the cupboard. She pulled out a half-eaten bag of plain potato chips. "Dang you and your detective's instincts."

"Detective instinct has nothing to do with it. That's big sister instinct knowing you won't eat a stick and slide sandwich without a glass of milk and potato chips. It's never happened in your entire life."

"Truth," Willow nodded her head like a reggae singer hearing a distant drum beat.

I made myself a sandwich and spent the next ten minutes happily crunching potato chips and eating the best sandwich I had tasted in weeks.

"Why are you two up?" I asked.

"We're going on a raid," Juliet said. She wrapped the bread up and returned the jars to their location on the shelves. All evidence of our middle of the night snack were soon cleared.

"A raid of what? The Alamo is at least five hundred miles to the east."

"We're going to raid my parents' personnel folders," Willow explained. "Dad thinks it's a huge betrayal of trust to suspect any of the staff. Mom thinks he should quit thinking like a hippie and protect his actual family. If my parents believed in yelling at each other, it would have happened tonight. It was the ugliest non-argument I've seen them have. The spirits are so sad."

"We decided to handle the matter ourselves, thereby absolving Harmony and Steve of any negative vibes."

"I don't know about the negative vibe absolution, but I'm all over looking at personnel files. I think that someone here knows more than what they are saying," I said.

"Then it's decided. Juliet and crew are on patrol." Juliet gave a fist pump and headed towards the door. When Willow and I didn't follow her, she turned and said, "Are you in or what?"

"I'm in," Willow said.

"I'm in, but I think it should be Phee and crew since I'm the oldest," I said.

"And the slowest, so get a move on granny," Juliet joked.

We switched off the kitchen lights and tiptoed our way down the hall. Willow was prepared because she pulled a penlight out of her dreadlocks and switched it on as we made our way to the office. The door was locked, but Willow pulled a set of keys from her robe.

"Mom leaves them hanging on a hook so Dad

doesn't accidentally wash them or lose them. The goddess will forgive me for my sticky fingers."

She quickly unlocked the door to the office and we slipped inside. I switched on the light and we quickly made our way to the bank of filing cabinets. Juliet reached to open one and I stopped her.

"I think we should let Willow comb through the files. It's her family's business."

Juliet nodded her agreement. Looking at personnel files was already a huge invasion of privacy. I certainly didn't want to see their personal or business financial records.

Willow flicked through the filing cabinet quickly and yanked out a stack of file folders. She put them onto the desk, and we all grabbed folders and began to read them.

Sandy Jimenez's file was on top. I skimmed through the file. She listed her next of kin as her mother, Pansy Jimenez. No other family was listed. She was only twenty-two. Her application said she was a part-time student at the university. Nothing incriminating in her file.

I flipped to the next file. Bridget Sullivan. She was the waitress who had found the body. I opened her file and saw that she was only seventeen and still in high school. I didn't think I would find much fodder for felony murder with her.

I closed her file after a minute's glance and looked to the next one. Antonio Bernardo, part-time groundskeeper and general handyman, had worked for Steve and Harmony for the past two years since before they even opened the spa. He listed his wife as his emergency contact. It looked like he had retired from a manufacturing plant in Texas before moving to Sedona. According to his application, he had wanted a part-time job so his wife wouldn't divorce him because he was bored out of his skull. Not necessarily what they recommend in Job Hunting 101, but it had clearly worked for him.

The final file in my stack was Marianne's. She had her last name listed as Hopewell, not Cassidy. No wonder Steve and Harmony hired Brad without talking to Marianne. They probably hadn't realized the two of them had a relationship to each other. She listed her sister as her next of kin and there was no mention of Brad in any of her employment records. Interesting, although not surprising if she was attempting to eradicate any memory of Brad and his philandering ways from her life. There was nothing else in her file that raised a red flag.

"I've got nothing interesting in any of my files. An ex-waitress who left for a higher paying job as a secretary in town, the sous chef had nothing exciting and neither did Kathy Whitestone's. This last file is for a girl named Megan who worked here as a maid for the summer before she left for university," Juliet said.

"All my files are run-of-the-mill, too," Willow

said with a resigned shake of her head. "I guess I didn't understand what the spirits were talking about. They aren't always clear."

"Hold on. These are all the files for past and present employees, right?" I asked.

"I think so. The resort is still on bare bones staffing until we get more guests staying here and Mom sees the bottom line a little healthier. She and Dad do a lot of stuff themselves or hire contractors to come in for the short term like Hari to teach classes."

"So, where's Brad's personnel file?" I asked.

"Maybe the police took it," Juliet said.

"Maybe. It's something we need to ask Harmony about. Don't give up on your spirits yet, Willow," I said. I stifled a yawn. "I need some sleep. Are we all done?"

"I guess so," Willow said, still looking discouraged.

We put the files back into the filing cabinet and got ready to leave. Willow shut off the light and locked the door behind us.

"I'll see you two in the morning." Willow yawned and trudged down the hallway to the family's living quarters.

Juliet and I began to tiptoe are way back to the guest rooms when I caught a flash of something at the end of the hall. I put my hand out to stop Juliet and pointed. Someone was walking around the spa area with a flashlight. I could tell by the way the light bobbed behind the frosted glass door. I ran on tiptoes down the hall towards the door trying to catch whoever was lurking around. I was just about to reach for the door when my foot caught on the edge of one of the rugs and I went flying. I landed with a loud thump as I made contact with the tile floor. The flashlight shut off.

"Dang it!" I hissed. I eased my way up from the floor, but almost fell back down as the pain shot through my ankle. "Holy guacamole that hurts!"

I stood up and gingerly tried to put my weight on my knee. It wasn't going to happen. Juliet moved up behind me. "Are you okay?"

"No, but don't worry about me. See if you can see who's in there."

Juliet tiptoed to the door and eased it open. She shuffled her body crablike to the edge of the door and then leaped around it and yelled, "Freeze, sucker!"

I rolled my eyes. I really needed to have an intervention for her before she got too crazy with her bad cop lingo.

Juliet peeked back around the door at me. "Nobody's in here. I'm going to check the treatment rooms."

"Wait for me." I limped my way after her. We checked the rooms but didn't find anything. Whoever it was had snuck out through the staff doors at the back of the spa. As we made our way back to the hallway, I had to stop and sit down.

"Are you going to survive?" Juliet asked and

knelt to look at my ankle. By now it had swelled to the size of a grapefruit and turned a lovely shade of purple and black. "Oh. That's not looking so good. Does it hurt?"

"Do ya think?" I growled at her. "I think I need a doctor."

"I think you're right. For now, let me get you back to your room. You can elevate your foot until I can get dressed and get a car to take you into town. Mom's going to be upset."

"It's not my fault I fell and hurt it."

"You know she gets all mother bear weird whenever one of us gets injured."

Juliet was right. Most moms would be solicitous of a child's injury or illness. Our mom went to such an extreme that we practically smothered under all the care and chicken soup she dished up. After the second day, we all prayed for a miracle healing just so we could rest and get some sleep without her watching us.

"Just get me to my room."

Juliet helped me hop my way up the stairs and to my room. She helped me get dressed in a pair of shorts and a clean t-shirt before heading back to her room to get dressed. Fifteen minutes later she was back and helping me hop my way back downstairs. Lu met us at the bottom of the stairs looking like a mountain lion who hadn't eaten in a month. She held up her hand and showed us the keys to Willow's car.

"Don't talk to me until I get some coffee," Lu

growled. "I don't know what you two were doing gallivanting around in the wee hours of the morning, but this is why Clint nags you two to leave the investigation to the professionals."

"We were hungry and went for a snack," Juliet protested.

Lu held up her hand for silence. "So, the food attacked you? You had to tackle the tofu and skin it before eating it? What?"

"I tripped trying to sneak up on somebody."

Lu gave me the hairy eyeball as she helped me into the front seat. "I rest my case. Every time you two start playing Nancy Clue, somebody gets shot or eaten by an alligator-"

"Drew," I corrected her.

"What?"

"It's Nancy Drew, not Clue," I said.

"Unbelievable," Lu snorted. She barely waited for Juliet to get into the car before slamming it into gear and heading towards town.

"Everyone's employment files were in the office, but Brad's," Juliet said. "Do you think Deputy McCall has it?"

"I don't know," Lu said. "Maybe I'll call him up at five a.m. and ask him. Never mind that it's not my jurisdiction, not my case, and not my business!"

"We're just trying to help Harmony and Steve," Juliet replied in a small, quiet voice.

Lu sighed and gave me a side glance. "I know. Listen. We are strangers in a strange land here, you two. We don't really know anyone and this place isn't like Miller's Cove where everyone knows everyone's business and babysat you when you were two. You can't go poking your nose into this one. Just leave it alone."

"We really did eat a snack," I said. "The tripping and falling trying to sneak up on the perp was an afterthought."

"Absolutely unbelievable." Lu snorted again and pressed her foot down on the accelerator as we made our way towards the hospital.

Two hours later, I was wrapped up in bandages and sporting a pair of crutches. My ankle was badly sprained, and I had strict instructions to take it easy. After begging Lu to take a side trip to a local café for some real food, we were all settled down at the Hungry Armadillo. I breathed in the rich smell of bacon frying on the grill as the waitress took our order.

Lu sipped at her cup of black coffee and after a moment, her face relaxed and a small grin appeared.

"What's so funny?" I asked.

"I can't believe you managed to get injured on vacation."

"It's a skill. Not everyone has it, but those of us who do, are experts."

"The good thing about your lack of mobility is it makes it impossible for you to nose around looking for a murderer."

"I can investigate," Juliet chimed in. "First

thing when we get back, I'm going to ask Harmony about Brad's file."

Thankfully, the waitress appeared with our food to keep Lu from tackling Juliet and handcuffing her to the table. I picked up the syrup and let its golden-brown liquid work its way across my pancakes before puddling in a gooey pool next to my bacon. There was silence at our table for the next several minutes as we participated in comfort food therapy.

"I have some ideas," I said. I mopped the last of my syrup up with my slice of bacon and popped it into my mouth. Heaven. "We assume that Brad was the prankster and somebody killed him because of it, right?"

"True," Juliet said slowly, "but the only people who would have a motive to kill him for that are Harmony and Steve. Willow was with them the afternoon of the murder, and the only way Steve could have killed him is by sending him negative vibes until he croaked."

"Harmony could do it," I said. "She's edgy, but she's smart. No way would she leave a body stashed on her own property. I think as far as Steve and Harmony were concerned, Brad was just a bad employee and they fired him – end of story."

"Makes sense." Lu sipped her coffee. "Let's change the dynamic. Brad wasn't the prankster. Someone else was trying to make the business fail and he got caught up in the action somehow. His murder is totally unrelated."

"Okay. We're back to square one – the original problem. Who wants Harmonious Healing to fail?"

"Easy," Juliet said. "Francine Whitaker and Idelia Riggs."

"Who are they?" Lu asked.

I quickly explained about the realtor and her sleazy plan to ruin the business and my theory that she and Idelia were behind the false story that the spa was built on sacred grounds.

"Francine has motive for the pranks and possibly opportunity if she has someone on the inside helping her out," Juliet said.

"Look at you thinking like a really detective instead of a pretend one," Lu gave her a shrewd look. "Impressive. I'll make a cop out of you yet."

Juliet preened like a chicken under Lu's praise. "I try."

"We need to find out if she or Idelia have any tie to Brad or not," I said. "But first, I'm going to get another rasher of bacon and another cup of coffee."

"Everything is better with bacon," Lu said, lifting her coffee cup to clink it with mine.

"You've got that right." Juliet chimed in.

"Says the girl who drinks green kale smoothies."

We finished up our breakfast and paid. As we headed out towards the car with Juliet giving me tips on crutch walking, Sheriff Martinez pulled up and headed towards the diner.

"You two go ahead to the car," Lu instructed. "I'll catch up with you in a minute."

"We want to talk to the sheriff, too," Juliet whined

One evil-eyed glare from Lu sent us all scampering to the car. Well, one of us scampered. I hobbled.

"What do you think they're talking about," Juliet asked as she tried to turn her head without being obvious to watch Lu and the sheriff talk.

"Cop stuff," I replied.

"Really?" Juliet gave me a scornful look.

"Well, I certainly don't think they are exchanging makeup tips," I shot back.

Lu waved goodbye to the sheriff and headed to the car. She climbed in without a word and started the car.

"What did she say?" Juliet panted from the backseat.

"Not much." Lu gave a noncommittal shrug.

"She didn't tell you about the case?"

"Not really?" Lu put the car into drive and pulled out into the street.

"Seriously? Didn't you ask her about Brad, the pranks, the murder, anything crime-related?" Juliet's voice went up a notch as her frustration level grew.

"We talked about the fact that it's a crime that women's shampoo costs twice as much as men's."

"Are you kidding me?" Juliet screeched.

Lu barked out a laugh. "You are so easy, Juliet. They don't have Brad Cassidy's personnel file, but they did make a copy of it. Marianne was asked to come identify the body and give a more formal statement, but she is not under arrest. Anything else you want to know?"

"Any family in the area?" I asked. Dang Willow's spirit guides for taking over the investigation.

"None other than Marianne. Satisfied?"

"Not really, but I guess you aren't as practiced in wearing down a person until they spill their dirtiest little secret that no one knows but them and the goddess," Juliet pouted.

"You're killing me, Juls. Absolutely killing me."

CHAPTER THIRTEEN

It was only nine o'clock when we got back to the resort. Willow was pacing in the dining room when we walked in.

"How in the goddess's good name did you sprain your ankle?" Willow's hands twisted the tree of life charm necklace she wore. "This vortex is sucking away my connection to my spirit guides. I need to get back to the forest and my stones. They should have warned me."

"The spirits probably forgot that I was such a klutz." I patted Willow on her shoulder. "I'm fine. In fact, I'm more than fine. I finally get to relax and read a book by the pool. Maybe my sister will be nice enough to run upstairs to my room and get my paperback so I can."

"I guess it won't kill me to help you out," Juliet sighed and did a dramatic dragging of her feet as she made her way up the stairs.

I made my way to the pool, and Willow brought me a pillow for my foot and a bottle of sunscreen for my face. Juliet made her way back downstairs holding my paperback mystery, sunglasses and my sunhat. I knew I didn't drop her on her head when she was a toddler for nothing. Sometimes baby sisters came in handy. She said she wanted to catch the mid-morning yoga class and promised she would check on me later.

I settled back and let the morning sun warm

me. I must have fell asleep because when I next looked at my paperback, it was on the ground next to my lounge chair. I leaned over to pick it up and noticed a scrap of paper wedged in the space between the bricks and the wrought iron fence surrounding the patio. I tugged, and it tore leaving me with a scrap of paper between my fingers. I looked at it closely. It was part of an envelope with a return address and part of the addressee's name. The envelope was addressed to a Megan Konner- from a Harriet Konner, 155 Milford Road, Mon- and the rest was missing. Someone must have lost it. I stuck it in my short pockets to throw away later.

I returned to my book and was soon lost in the adventures of Chee and Leaphorn. It was great being in the midst of the Arizona desert while reading a mystery set in the Arizona desert. Non-readers had no idea the great adventures they were missing. I gave a contented sigh. Now this was a vacation.

I was happily engrossed in my book when I heard a woman speaking in an urgent, low voice behind me. Someone was on the other side of the fence. I wanted to turn around, but if I peeked over the top of my lounge chair, they would realize I was there. I didn't want anyone to think I was eavesdropping even if I was.

"That's normal for this stage, honey," the woman said. "I'm sure if anything was wrong, the doctor would tell you. And stretch marks are badges of honor. We all get them at some point. I call mine tiger stripes. Try to stop worrying. You'll have enough to worry about once the baby comes. Trust me. You ran me ragged as a toddler."

That was sweet. A mom reassuring their pregnant daughter. The woman's voice faded as she moved away from the fence. I spun around and caught the back of a taller woman with long hair whose pale strands glinted in the sun, but at this angle, I couldn't tell which of my fellow guests it was. I was guessing it was the geologist since she was the only guest staying here that was old enough to be expecting a grandchild. The blue-haired ladies had departed the day before.

I decided I had better get out of the sun before my pale tan I had acquired over the past few days turned lobster red. I picked up my crutches, stuffed my paperback into my waistband and worked my way back inside. Fortunately, the resort had a small elevator which quickly took me to the second floor. Once I got in my room, I decided I needed to take a shower. I was sweaty from sitting in the sun. But I had a wrapped foot that I couldn't get wet. I sighed and picked up my cell phone and texted Juliet

Ten minutes later, there was a light tap on my door. I hopped my way over to let her in. She stood leaning in against the doorjamb with a plastic grocery bag in one hand and a bungee cord in the other.

"What do you plan on doing with that?" I said, my eyes wide with fear. "Strap me onto the roof of the Jeep and hose me down?"

"No, silly. I am going to put the grocery bag around your foot and wrap the bungee cord around your calf. Voila! You can shower without getting your bandage wet. This," she motioned to her face, "is more than a pretty face. There is a functioning and creative being behind these eyes."

"Thank goodness because for a moment I was worried that I really had gotten *all* the brains in this family."

Juliet gave me a dirty look but helped me into the grocery bag and tightened the cord. "I'm going to go hang out with Willow. Come downstairs when you're done."

I showered and felt one hundred and ten percent better. I dressed in a clean pair of shorts and a loose aqua t-shirt and put one sandal on. There better not be any creepy crawlies between me and the floor.

I found Willow and Juliet playing a game of checkers in the lounge area. Soft music played in the background and I recognized a Guns-N-Roses' *Sweet Child of Mine*, but it was just wrong when played on a flute with a New Age beat to it.

"Welcome to the land of the living, Phee. The spirits sent best wishes for quick healing of your injured ankle."

"Tell the spirits I said thanks."

"Marianne's in the office with Mom and Dad. We're waiting to see what she has to say."

"And then hit her with the third degree on her relationship with Brad," Juliet added.

"Ahem. I want to offer her a healing pouch with power stones. I think she'll find they bring her comfort."

"Oh. You don't think she's quitting, do you? It's not her fault her ex-husband was murdered," I said.

"Or is it?" Juliet raised her eyebrow.

"We don't know who did it yet, Judge Jul. Not enough evidence or did you forget that part." I wagged an admonishing finger at her.

The door to the office opened and Marianne came out teary-eyed. Harmony and Steve each gave her a hug.

Willow stood up and walked towards her. She embraced her and handed her a bright blue pouch tied with brown twine with a twig of lavender. "The spirits hope these stones will give you healing in your time of trouble."

"Uh…thanks?" Marianne took the offered gift and put it in her purse.

Juliet took the opportunity to insert herself into the mix. "How are you doing, Marianne? Okay? I was sorry to hear about your husband." She looked over her shoulder at me and winked.

"Ex-husband. I'm not crying over him. I stopped crying over him months ago."

"Really? Brad wasn't a nice guy?" Juliet placed

her arm around Marianne's shoulder and guided her to the couch next to me.

"Oh, he was nice. He was nice to every woman under the age of thirty. That's why he's my ex."

"I met Luke," I said. "He seems nice."

Marianne's face brightened at the mention of Luke's name. "He's a great guy. Considerate. Loyal. Faithful."

"The police don't think you killed Brad do they?" Juliet said innocently.

"I don't think so. They told me I can't leave town, but where would I go? My home, my job, my fiancé are here in Sedona. I left my old life behind when I moved to Sedona. At least I thought I had until he showed up here at Harmonious Healing."

"Why did he come to Sedona? Was it to try to reconcile with you?" I asked.

Marianne snorted. "The only reason he showed his sorry face near me and acted like he wanted to reconcile was to try to steal my grandma's inheritance from me. I saw through that charade and saw through his cock and bull story that he was a changed man."

"I did hear that he was caught peeking at the ladies." Juliet shook her sadly in her best imitation of girl camaraderie. "Some men are such pigs."

"It was more than just peeking at the female guests. He was caught messing around with one of the young girls who worked here. That's just gross. He was knocking on thirty years old and chasing after a teenager."

"Sounds like you had a lot of anger at him," I said.

Marianne eyed me warily. "You sound like the deputy. Was I angry at Brad? Yes. Did I hate his guts sometimes? Yes. Was I angry enough to kill him? No. I had moved on and so had he."

"I heard he had moved away for a job after he got fired from here. How come he was back?" Willow asked.

"He came back a week ago. I was hot that he had the nerve to show back up in Sedona. I ran into him at the Hungry Armadillo and confronted him. He said it wasn't about me. Brad said he came here to make things right and said it was a family matter. I don't know how that's possible since his family lives in California."

Willow gave me a wide-eyed look and said, "The spirits were right!"

Heaven help me, but Willow's spirits might be onto something. If only we knew what it was.

CHAPTER FOURTEEN

Since I couldn't really do much walking and sightseeing, Juliet and I decided today was the perfect day for pedicures and manicures. The spa had a couple of cancellations because of the murder, so Sandy's schedule was empty for the afternoon. Juliet and Lu climbed into the spa's loungers and let the foot spas soften their feet while I had my nails manicured.

"How are you, Sandy?" I asked.

She was buffing my short nails into some semblance of shape and took a moment to answer. "I'm okay, I guess. My mom wants me to quit because of the murder, but I like this job. Harmony and Steve work with my school schedule. Mom wants me to quit and go to work full-time at the casino, but then I couldn't go to college. Money's tight at our house, but I don't want to stop going to school."

"Once you get your degree, you'll be able to get a better paying job and really help your mom out. An education is important." As I said the words I realized how hollow they sounded. When you had to decide whether to pay the electric bill or pay for a textbook, saying that an education was important sounded elitist.

Sandy didn't seem to notice my awkward pause. "I know that and she knows that, but it's hard sometimes. Harmony said once I finish my degree, she'll promote me to manager. She said by then the spa should be busier and she can afford to pay me more since I'll have more responsibility."

We sat quietly while she worked on my ragged cuticles. Once she started applying the bright pink polish I had chosen, I decided to probe a little bit more.

"Have you talked to Marianne?" I asked.

"Not really. Like I said before, we aren't super close or anything. The drama with Brad ate up most of her free time and energy, so we never really had a chance to hang out."

"I heard that Brad had a wandering eye with the ladies. A real ladies' man. Did he ever try anything with you?" I felt like I was being pushy, but at this point, what did I have to lose? If I didn't ask, Juliet would.

"Kind of," Sandy said. She was concentrating on my nails, so I couldn't see her face. "I mean, I'm not really his type."

She wasn't going to make this easy. "What do you mean?"

"Well, I heard that he liked blondes. My dark hair and skin probably turned him off. Not that I'm complaining. I didn't want some old married guy creeping in on me."

Brad was only twenty-nine, so I must fall into the old category, too. I wondered if I had gray hair sprouting that I wasn't aware of.

She didn't say anything else after that and I didn't want to push things. She finished up my nails and I hobbled to the couch to read a magazine while she did Lu's and Juliet's nails.

"Haven't you ever had a pedicure?" Juliet asked Lu.

"Once. It weirded me out because it was a guy doing it. I haven't been back since. I polish my toes myself."

"You could have Anthony polish your toenails if you are feeling a little sassy and sexy," Juliet suggested slyly. "How is tall, redheaded and sexy?"

"He's good," Lu said noncommittally.

"Hmm…that's what I heard." Juliet poked the bear again.

"What? Who said that? Has he been seeing somebody else? I'll shoot him!" Lu jumped up and the water in the footbath sloshed around her.

"Settle down," Juliet laughed. "I was joking. Good to see you getting your dander up over a guy. I was scared you were an emotional desert."

"I'm reserved with my public displays of affection. Anthony is the drama king in this relationship. I prefer to be the low-key queen."

Sandy had been watching the back and forth between Juliet and Lu with amusement. "You had me scared when you threatened to shoot someone," Sandy joked nervously.

"I wasn't joking. I'm a cop with a gun and I'm not afraid to use it," Lu said with a deadpan expression before laughing and sitting back down in her massaging chair.

"You're police?" Sandy said with what seemed to me a hint of nervousness.

"Yup. Got a badge, a gun and a uniform back home that says so."

"Cool," Sandy answered. She went back to rubbing lotion on Juliet's feet.

I went back to reading my magazine and about thirty minutes later, the two of them were done. We decided since I was out of commission, they would leave me in peace to relax in the lounge and read a book and they would go hike around at another vortex. They left me with another book and went in search of Willow.

A short time later, the female geologist came into the lounge and settled down in a chair opposite me. I could feel her staring at me, so I put my book down and smiled at her.

"Hi. I'm Phee."

"Jennifer Johnson. Nice to meet you." She leaned forward and shook my hand. Her grasp was dry and rough and I could tell she spent time working with her hands.

"You're a geologist?"

"Sure am. I'm out here studying the alluvial fans."

"Sounds interesting," I said, not knowing for the life of me what an alluvial fan was, but I also wasn't into rocks.

"Maybe to geologists and volcanologists. I'm about as exciting as an accountant at my husband's corporate functions, but I find geology fascinating."

"I'm a librarian. I get told every day that I'm a dinosaur and my job is about to go extinct."

We sat there in awkward silence. I didn't know what she wanted, and I got the distinct feeling she was n and I got the distinct feeling she was nervous to ask.

"So…you and your husband came here specifically for you to study the Aleutian fans?"

"Alluvial." She corrected. "Not really. We came to Arizona so I could, but here to Harmonious Healing? No. My husband's treating me to his idea of a girl's luxury vacation. Even after twenty years of marriage he still has no idea what to get me for my birthday and his secretary always suggests something she would like but is so completely opposite of me it's hilarious."

"Why don't you drop a hint to the secretary?"

"I would, but then Phil would know that I know that he's never picked out my gifts and then he'd be heartbroken. I pretend to be thrilled and then use or wear the gift a few times before it conveniently disappears to the back of the closet. This time there was no way to put a spa vacation in the back of the closet."

"That's sweet," I said.

"It's what you do when you love someone," Jennifer said with a wry grin.

"I'm here with my sister, Juliet. She's getting married soon, so Harmony and Steve offered to let us stay here for a girls' getaway."

Jennifer sat for a moment, started to speak, stopped and then started again. "What do you know about the death that occurred here?"

I was at a loss for how to answer her. If I was staying here and didn't know the owners, I would want to know what was going on. But I also didn't want to hurt the investigation or betray Steve and Harmony.

"It was an ex-employee that was killed."

"Are we in danger?"

I thought about it. So far, nothing that happened pointed to anyone else being in danger. "I don't think so. I think it was a crime related to something this guy did. That's all I feel comfortable saying."

She leaned back with a relieved look. "That's good enough for me, but Phil's been a nervous wreck. He was suggesting we try to find another resort or fly to Florida for the rest of the week. The last thing I need is him insisting I start the pampering all over again."

I chuckled. She reminded me of Lu and her distaste of all the overtly girly things. One time I suggested Lu get a pink gun, and it was a week before she spoke to me again.

"Do you and your husband have any children?"

"No. By the time I was finished with my doctorate, I didn't want to take time off from any research. Kids aren't really my thing. My husband has four siblings who all have kids, so we get to play the indulgent aunt and uncle. The plus side is we get to give them back when they get cranky. It's a win-win situation."

"Sounds like it." I picked up my book.

"I had better go find Phil before he books me for a Vitamin C peel or a veggie cleanse. Or is it a Vitamin C cleanse and a veggie peel? Whatever. Nice meeting you."

I sat there after she left and worried about Harmony and Steve. What would they do if their business failed? Would they have to move to Miller's Cove and start over? Would Steve go into spiritual healing with Willow? I don't think Miller's Cove could handle two of them.

Despite the morning's huge breakfast, I was feeling the gnaw of hunger. I decided a snack was in order. I made my way over to the plate of cookies Willow said the kitchen baked fresh every day and left out for guests. I picked out a chocolate chip cookie from the pile of oatmeal raisin. The worst experience of my cookie life was when I bit into an oatmeal raisin cookie expecting chocolate chip. My mom said I cried for an hour until she baked a batch of chocolate chip cookies just for me. I was five at the time and I'm still scarred by the trauma.

I bit into the cookie and chewed. It was horrible and hot! I spat it out into the nearby trashcan. I hopped over to the water pitcher, poured myself a cup, and gulped it down.

I inspected the remaining bit of cookie still in

my hand. It had bits of green in it. Jalapenos and salt. That had to be what the taste in my mouth was. I loved jalapenos, but not like that. Did the chef try out a new recipe? I didn't know, but I was determined to find out.

I grabbed my crutches and made my way to the kitchen. I swung the door open but didn't go in due to the frenetic pace and energy of the place.

Chef Whitestone looked up from the sauce she was whisking. "Hey, Phee, what's going on? Is everything okay?"

"Can I ask you a question, Chef Whitestone?"

"Please call me Kathy. Ask away."

"I don't want you to think I'm criticizing your cooking or anything, but the cookies in the dining room are awful."

"Really? I made them using my grandma's cookie recipes this morning. I've made them a million times and everyone's always loved them." Kathy's face scrunched up in confusion.

"Maybe it's me then. I don't care for jalapenos in my cookies, especially when I think they are chocolate chip. No offense."

"None taken because I don't put jalapenos in cookies. Some things are sacred and my granny's cookie recipes are at the top of the list."

Kathy handed the bowl she was holding to the waitress, Bridget, and told her to keep whisking. She wiped her hands on her apron and motioned for me to follow her. We made our way back to the infamous plate of cookies. She picked one up, bit into it and immediately spat it out into her hand.

"That is by far the most awful tasting thing I've ever put in my mouth!" She picked up one of the oatmeal raisin cookies and bit into it. She chewed for a second then swallowed. "The oatmeal raisin cookies are fine. Someone's tampered with my granny's cookies!"

"Tampering with a grandma's cookie recipe is a crime that should be punishable with jail time," I said.

I picked up an oatmeal raisin to make Kathy feel better. It wasn't chocolate chip, but I was trying to expand my horizons. An oatmeal raisin here, a romance novel there. I was becoming a regular Renaissance woman.

"I'm going to get to the bottom of this. First a dead body in my freezer, and now bad cookies? What is the world coming to?"

"I don't know."

"I'll make it up to you tonight, Phee. I'll give you an extra big veggie tofu burrito."

"Oh, don't feel like you have to go out of your way. I'm fine."

Kathy waved off my protest, snatched up the remaining cookies and marched back to the kitchen in search of a cookie criminal. I wondered if I could drive to town to get a real burrito with a sprained ankle. Better yet, I wondered if any restaurants in town delivered to the spa.

CHAPTER FIFTEEN

I was holed up in my room eating my contraband chicken enchiladas and chile rellenos with green sauce when I heard a knock on my door.

"Let me in, Phee," Juliet said. "I can smell Mexican food through the door."

I put my food on the nightstand and said through the door, "How do I know it's you and not just some starving vegetarian who has finally snapped and come to steal my tasty dinner."

"You know my voice."

"You could be a vegetarian mimic pretending to be my sister."

"Ophelia Jefferson, let me in this room or I'm calling your mother."

I opened the door to let her in. "She's your mother, too."

"Yeah, well, she does like me better."

"No, she doesn't. She only told you that so you would get over your inferiority complex."

"What inferiority complex?"

"Exactly." I hopped back to the bed and picked up my food.

Juliet sniffed appreciatively and stole a chip from the container of chips and salsa sitting on the bed.

I poked her hand with my fork. "Get your own secret stash of food. I'm overcoming a traumatic experience. Someone sabotaged granny's cookies."

"Granny?"

"Chef Whitestone's cookies that she made from her grandmother's recipe were spiked with salt and jalapenos, and I ate one!"

"That doesn't even sound good."

"It wasn't, thus my comfort food smorgasbord. How was your hike with Lu?"

"Fun, but Lu's not feeling well. She said she had an upset stomach this morning, too. She decided to go up to her room and rest. She asked if I would bring her some dinner later this evening."

"I'm not eating tofu burritos. I don't have it in me to recover from that experience. I love Mexican food and some things should not be tampered with."

"Like cookies," Juliet said, as she stole another chip.

"Exactly like cookies. I might not be able to eat another chocolate chip cookie for weeks."

"I'm sure you'll be okay. You know what this means, don't you?"

"What?" I asked.

"The prankster is still around and it wasn't Brad. Now the question remains – are the two related or not?"

Juliet was right. Brad was dead and someone was still creating chaos.

"Let me finish my sinfully delicious chicken-filled dinner and I'll come downstairs with you," I said.

"If you share with me, you'll get done faster," Juliet said, eyeing my chile rellenos with a look like a hungry wolf eyeing a rabbit.

Sighing, I pulled another fork out of the bag the food came in and handed it to her. "Mom said it's important to share with your sister, but I thought that ended once we moved out."

"Not when it comes to Mexican food. You know I can't resist cheese and red sauce."

We finished up my dinner, and I brushed my hair up into a tight ponytail. The one benefit to being in the desert was my hair didn't frizz as much.

We made our way down to the lounge area where Harmony and Steve had set up a small wine bar with appetizers for the guests. There were a few new faces – a couple from Florida, Jackie and Jon, who were working their way to California who decided to stay until the weekend, and an older woman named Patricia who said she came to Sedona twice a year for a break from caring for her mother who was in her nineties and bedridden.

"My daughter takes over, so that I can have a mental health break," Patricia explained.

Juliet and I mingled with the new group while we waited for Willow. Lu was still not feeling well and wanted to have a video chat date with Anthony instead of dinner.

I noticed two older women had joined come

into the lounge. One of the women was clearly of Native American heritage and wore a large squash blossom necklace and had her dark hair pulled back into a tight braid. The other woman looked familiar. She had blonde hair cropped short and her jewelry, dress, shoes and purse were color-coordinated. When I looked closer, I realized that even her lipstick matched her outfit. That was a skill I hoped I would never learn nor need.

"That's Francine Whitaker," I whispered to Juliet. "I recognize her from the life-size cutout they had of her at the real estate office. I wonder if that's Idelia Riggs with her."

"I've got this," Juliet said. She refilled her wine glass with some of the chilled white wine and waltzed her way over to Francine. Since I was on crutches, I couldn't waltz. I crutched it instead causing wine to splash on my hand.

"Hi. Juliet Jefferson." Juliet stretched out her hand to Francine.

Francine, ever the salesperson, put on a large, blindingly white-toothed smile and shook her hand. In a deep Southern drawl, she said, "Francine Whitaker, real estate agent, and this is my colleague, Idelia Riggs."

Juliet turned to Idelia. "You're in real estate, too."

"I, uh, I...not really...I help Francine when she needs me," Idelia stuttered in response. She did not take Juliet's hand nor did the dour expression on her face crack.

"Real estate must be booming in Sedona if you need an assistant. I briefly considered going into real estate myself, but I discovered I didn't have the personality for sales," Juliet hesitated briefly on the word personality.

"Oh, honey, you've got to be a go-getter in this field if you're going to survive. It's like I tell Idelia. If you want something, you just put on your big girl panties and go after it. Ain't time to pussyfoot around things."

"Sounds like you're a go-getter, alright. This is my sister, Ophelia." Juliet turned to me.

"Nice to meet you. Are you friends with Harmony and Steve?" I asked.

"We're really good friends," Francine said with her shark-toothed grin. "I'm here on business today. I'm like Martha Stewart. Just go, go, go. No time for sleep when there are deals to be made. Now, if you girls will excuse me, I'm going to go say hi to Steve over there."

Francine left us in a cloud of expensive perfume and strode over to Steve who looked like a dog trapped at the pound with no hope of rescue. Idelia scowled after Francine.

"So," I said, "aside from helping Francine with real estate, what else do you do, Idelia?"

"I'm on the tribal council. All these tourists traipsing all over our sacred land keeps me busy."

"Sounds interesting," I nodded my head and ignored the not-so-subtle jibe against my tourist status. "I guess you heard about the trouble Steve and Harmony had a few days ago."

Idelia snorted. "It was all over town before the cops even returned to their office. Steve and Harmony may as well hang up the closed sign and leave town. There's no way this place will survive after someone was killed here. Serves them right."

"That's a little harsh, don't you think?" Juliet asked. "Did you know Brad Cassidy?"

Idelia let out another snort. "Any woman under the age of fifty knew Brad Cassidy. The man hit on everybody. Personally, I don't blame his wife for killing him. It couldn't have happened to a more deserving individual."

"It sounds like you could have killed him yourself." Juliet wasn't pulling any punches.

Idelia let out a raspberry of disgust. "Me? I met the man twice. Didn't know him enough to want him dead. I just heard all the rumors and felt bad for his wife. Besides, I was over at Standing Rock until this morning. I heard about the murder from my sister. She knows all the gossip."

"Did Francine have a lot of interaction with Brad?" I asked.

"Do I look like her secretary? If you want to know about Francine, ask Francine."

This woman was as prickly as a porcupine sitting on a cactus. I hoped she wasn't the public relations person for the tribal council because if so, they were in deep trouble.

"I was at the museum yesterday and learned some fascinating information about the area. Are you a member of the Yavapai tribe?" I asked.

"Yes. Don't believe that line of old white man history that crank Butters fed you. My people's history isn't out there for entertainment and inspection. We have a strong oral history, but that doesn't fit in with Dr. Butters' plan, so it isn't deemed worthy of acknowledgement." Idelia's lip curled derisively when she said Dr. Butters' name.

"Um...okay. He said that this area wasn't considered sacred to your tribe." I backed away slightly behind Juliet. This woman scared me with her overt anger at the world.

"Like he's an expert on the sacred sites of our tribe. Give me a break. Maybe I should go build a casino hall on top of one of your church cemeteries. Not so great, then, is it?" She spat the words at us then turned and stalked over to Francine.

Harmony now stood next to Steve. I wasn't sure what was going on, but it couldn't be good. Harmony's face was stark white and tight and her eyes had narrowed with anger. If I didn't know any better, I could have sworn she planned on punching Francine.

Francine gave Harmony and Steve a bright smile and said, "You think about it. It's a good offer and after the week you've had, I doubt you'll get another one. Tootles."

Francine turned on her blue pumps and walked towards the door with Idelia trailing grumpily behind her.

"That woman has bad karma coming," a voice said from behind me.

Startled, I sloshed more of my wine. At this rate, I would need a refill before I even drank half a glass. I turned to see Hari standing behind me. She held a glass of ice water with a lime floating in it.

"Hi, Hari. You startled me."

"Sorry about that. Phee, wasn't it?" Hari's pale eyes assessed my crutches and bandaged foot.

"Yes. Juliet's sister."

"Spa accident?" She pointed to my foot.

"I twisted my ankle last night when I tripped."

"You can do yoga in a chair. Perhaps you should join my class tomorrow morning. It may bring a new awareness to your existence."

"I will." I gulped. This woman was intense. I didn't dare turn her suggestion down for fear of bad karma. After the jeep breaking down, the sprained ankle and bad cookies, I couldn't afford the universe to dish out any more karma. "Do you live near the resort."

Hari gave a small smile. "I live in California. I stay here at the resort for a few months at a time teaching classes and then head back home to work at another spa there, write, and reconnect my spirit to the earth."

"I didn't realize you were part of the staff."

"I'm not. Steve and I have an understanding. Nothing so crass as an employment contract. I like it here. Sedona has good vibes."

"The vibes were a little toxic the other night with Brad dying," Juliet said.

"Perhaps his karma finally caught up with him," Hari said in a clipped voice before she swirled away in the sea of her long skirt, scarf and silver hair.

Dang. Whatever happened to karmic love for the universe, peace on earth and goodwill towards men, I thought.

CHAPTER SIXTEEN

Juliet and I walked over to Willow and her parents. Harmony was still white-faced from her encounter with Francine.

"Now, Honey Bear, you shouldn't let her get under your skin," Steve admonished. "You know she gets your aura all red."

"I could kill her," Harmony said through tight lips.

"Mom!" Willow said in a shocked voice, then lowered it. "Don't say things like that. Especially since Brad was murdered here. It's bad for business and bad for your celestial future."

"Celestial future be damned!" Harmony exclaimed. A couple of the guests looked at our group, but quickly went back to their conversations. Harmony lowered her voice. "You're right, but that woman makes me so angry! How dare she try to capitalize on Brad's murder to give us a lowball offer on the spa."

"You're not going to consider it, are you?" Willow asked.

"Certainly not. I'm made of sterner stuff than Francine Whitaker and it will be a cold day in Sedona before I sell to anyone she brings to the table."

"Good," Willow said. "The spirits told me that this place is going to be successful one day if you and dad can stay strong. I'm going to brew a batch of tea this evening to help bring greater clarity. Phee? Juliet? Do you want to join us this evening?"

My eyes grew wide with fear. I had drank some of Willow's special brews before and I was not up for a repeat of the experience.

"Sorry, Willow, but I'm exhausted and my ankle hurts. But I'm sure Juliet would love to join you for your tea."

Juliet rolled her eyes at me and stuck out her tongue. Serves my hippie dippy sister right for making me drink a kale and wheat grass smoothie a few weeks ago. My taste buds were still in recovery.

I bid everyone goodnight and said I would see them in the morning. I really was tired. I made my way down the hall to the elevator. As I stepped onto the elevator, I spotted Hari out of the corner of my eye. She had her cell phone to her ear and was in an urgent conversation with someone. Before I could listen in, the door swished shut and I was whisked upwards to my room.

I sighed. I hated thinking suspicious thoughts about everyone I met. It was emotionally exhausting. I was taking a page out of Lu's book and turning in early.

I awoke the next morning to my ringing cell phone. I fumbled to unplug it from the charger and answer it.

"Hello?"

"Good morning, beautiful," a low, husky voice

said. "This is your wake-up call to tell you I miss you."

"Good morning." I hoped Clint could hear the smile in my voice. What a great way to wake up.

"How's the ankle?"

"It's still there." I yawned and sat up.

"That's good. I would hate to have a girlfriend with great legs, but only one ankle."

"You'd get used to it. I can't believe I slept for twelve hours straight. I went right to sleep after hanging up with you last night."

"Tripping over air and solving crimes can be exhausting," Clint said with a chuckle.

"You and my sister with the comedy act. Speaking of which, how's my future brother-in-law holding up with both his boss and his fiancée gone?"

"Wade's fine. He stopped by the house last night and we drank beer and ate thick, unhealthy steaks."

"That's okay. I ordered takeout and had it delivered here to the resort. I couldn't take a tofu burrito."

"That's just blasphemous."

"I know. I'll be home in two days and I expect you to cook me a thick, unhealthy burger with extra fries on the side."

"I can't wait to see you."

"I can't wait to kiss you," Clint responded. "Bye, love."

I hung up and snuggled back under the covers.

I loved that man. I shivered with happiness. I wondered if I could talk him in to taking a day off from work to spend it with me at home once I got back. If it took a little convincing, that would be half the fun.

I stayed in bed wrapped up in my thoughts for a few minutes longer before getting up. I stepped out of bed, forgetting my sprained ankle, and immediately, pain shot through me.

I sat back down. I took a deep breath, grabbed the crutches from where they leaned against the wall and made my way to the bathroom where I wrestled Juliet's plastic bag and bungee contraption over my ankle so I could shower.

Twenty minutes later, I was dressed in yoga pants and a sleeveless shirt. After last night's fattening dinner, I decided a little chair yoga couldn't hurt. I had a bridesmaid's dress to look good in. At least, I hope I did. If Juliet decided to have a wedding in the nude, I would have to bail on my sister and her wedding. There were some things even family couldn't expect me to do.

I was downstairs drinking a cup of coffee when Juliet made an appearance. She looked a little worse for the wear which for my gorgeous sister meant she had a hair out of place.

"What happened to you?" I asked.

"A bottle of wine with Willow followed by her healing energy sludge. I don't know which is hurting me worse – the wine or the tea."

I poured her a cup of coffee from the carafe in

front of me. "Drink up. Yoga starts in fifteen minutes and I'm in with the chair and my downward dog."

"Oh, good gravy."

She sipped her coffee and after a few minutes, she seemed back to her old, perky self. "I can't believe Francine had the nerve to show her face around here. Pushing Steve and Harmony to sell this place is dirty dealings as far as I'm concerned. I want to know why she needs this place so badly."

"I think we need to make a trip into town to do a little thing I like to call reference work or in non-librarian parlance, research. Maybe there's some history or something special about this land that makes it valuable."

"It's rocks and desert."

"It might be rocks and desert to us, but to someone else it could be sacred rocks and desert. Who knows."

"I'm in, but you have to do that spinning machine that makes me get vertigo," Juliet said.

"You mean the microfilm machine?"

"Yeah. It's the devil on my eyes and brain. All those images swimming past at a high rate of speed makes me nauseous."

"Fine. I'm on microfilm. Now let's get to class before we're late."

We walked outside to the yoga class. Juliet grabbed one of the pink yoga mats out of the bin and rolled it out on the grass. She pulled a chair from the patio and placed it next to her mat so I could join in.

Patricia, Jackie, Willow, Steve, and Phil, the geologist's husband, were already waiting on their mats when Hari arrived looking flustered. She rushed in and grabbed a mat before acknowledging her students were there.

"Good morning, everyone. Thank you for being punctual," Hari said, in a low, soothing voice. "As we begin our practice this morning, I want you to imagine that you are next to a river. As you work your way through each movement, each salutation, imagine that you are releasing your worries into the river like a lotus flower and watching it float away on the ripples."

I closed my eyes and imagined a river. As I raised my hands upward in my modified mountain pose, I imagined that my worries about Brad, the upcoming wedding and my small library budget were flowers floating away on the water. It did make me feel better and I felt my shoulders relaxed as we continued our practice.

Afterwards, Hari came up and put a warm hand on my shoulder. "I'm so glad you joined us today, Phee. I find yoga soothes the worries that weigh on my heart."

"I do feel better. Thank you."

Hari gave me a smile that didn't quite reach her pale eyes and walked over to Steve. The two of them were soon engaged in an animated discussion over different yoga practices. Willow excused herself and walked over to me.

"Where's Lu?" she asked.

"No clue. Juliet, did you talk to Lu this morning?"

"I knocked on her door, but she didn't answer. She's probably tired. I know she was feeling cruddy yesterday. I'll go upstairs and check on her."

I tried to hoist myself out of my chair, but lost my balance and plopped back down in my seat. Willow laughed and held out her hand to help me. "You better ice that ankle. I know when I sprained mine a few years back rock climbing, the doctor wanted me to ice it twice a day. Why don't you see if Chef Whitestone will lend you one of her ice packs?"

"Good idea. I'll do that." I grabbed Willow's hand and stood up. She handed me my crutches. "Juliet, I'm going to go get an ice pack. Meet me in the dining room in fifteen minutes for breakfast?"

"Make it twenty. I was running so late this morning, I didn't have time to shower. Plus, I want to check on Lu."

I made my way to the kitchen. Kathy was leaning against the counter sipping coffee, but when I walked in she straightened up and put her cup down.

"Keep drinking your coffee. I only came in to see if I could get an icepack from you to put on my ankle."

"Take whichever one you want out of the freezer. I have about five sitting on the shelf right inside the door."

"Thanks."

Kathy started to pick up her coffee cup, but the waitress walked in and stuck an order on the spinner.

"Order in, chef."

Kathy sighed. "A chef's work is never done."

I laughed. I went to the back of the kitchen to the walk-in freezer. I didn't want to go in there since Brad's body had been found in there. I wondered if they threw out all the food. I guess if the dead cooties hadn't touched it, it was probably good, but I wouldn't be eating couscous anytime soon.

I steeled my nerve and opened the door. I walked in and spotted the icepacks in a metal pan on a set of shelves on the left side of the freezer. I had to walk all the way in to reach them. The door closed behind me and I shivered for a minute. I didn't look at the corner of the freezer where Brad's body had lain. Grabbing an icepack from the pan, I turned and grabbed the door. The handle wouldn't push in like it normally should. I'd worked as a waitress in college and all these deep freezers had safety features to keep people from getting locked in them. I pushed harder and it wouldn't budge. I banged on the door and looked through the small, rectangular window, but Kathy had her back to me.

"Juliet better come looking for me before I become a human popsicle with hair," I said to the giant tub of green chile sauce next to me.

I sat down on one of the sealed white buckets and waited for rescue. After a minute, I started to feel the cold creeping into my skin and causing goose bumps. Juliet's shower better be short.

I darted my eyes to where Brad had died. Why would Brad have come into the freezer? Did he come to get food? An ice pack? Was he killed in the freezer or was his body just tucked in there until a more convenient spot could be found. There didn't seem to be any bloodstains anywhere, but I guessed there wouldn't be on stainless steel.

I rubbed my arms and attempted to warm myself. I wouldn't need an icepack after this because my ankle would be iced enough for a week. I let that happy thought warm me for a minute. I started to hum in an attempt to distract myself. I would have done jumping jacks to warm up but couldn't because I had fallen over a rug. Juliet better bring me chocolate chip cookies for a month after this vacation fiasco. Then I felt bad. I was a horrible sister. This was supposed to be her girls' getaway before her wedding. It was ruined by a dead body and here I was, her maid of honor, sitting here in a freezer feeling sorry for myself. I was a bad sister.

Fifteen minutes later, the freezer door opened and Juliet stood there. "Oh, my gosh, Phee! Are you okay?"

"I'm grand," I chattered. "Just a little chilly."

Juliet rushed in and helped me up. She grabbed my crutches, and I held on to her as I hopped my way out of the freezer.

"What happened?" Kathy asked as she rushed up to where we stood.

"I went into the freezer for the icepack and the door shut behind me. It wouldn't open," I said, lips stiff with cold.

Kathy rushed over to the counter and poured me a cup of coffee. She handed it to me and said, "Drink."

I took a swallow with my teeth clattering against the china. I cringed at the bitter taste of black coffee, but took another few swallows before I finally felt some warmth creeping back through me.

"I don't know who is behind these jokes, but if I find them, I'm going to kill them myself," Juliet swore.

"I don't understand. This freezer has a safety mechanism guaranteed to be tamper-proof." Kathy walked over to the freezer and opened the door. She lifted the handle up and it moved easily. "Huh. It seems to be working fine now. Nobody else was in the kitchen but Bridget and me this morning. Breakfast is slow, so I usually handle it myself."

I gave her a sheepish look. "I pushed it."

"What?" Kathy gave me a confused look.

"I pushed the handle. I didn't lift it. I probably could have gotten out the whole time." I gave her an apologetic smile.

"Holy jalapenos! I am the family genius!" Juliet exclaimed.

I rolled my eyes. "Get me to a warm, sunny spot and bring me coffee, woman. Be the family genius and waitress because your sister is a Pheesicle."

Juliet laughed. "A Pheesicle. Good one."

She handed me my crutches, and we made our way to the dining room. She brought me a cup and a full carafe of coffee. "Look. I even brought you a banana chocolate chip muffin. You love banana chocolate chip."

"I do," I sniffled. She really was a great sister. "I love you, Juls."

"What did you do?" Juliet eyed me suspiciously.

"Nothing. I feel bad that your big hurrah before your wedding has been ruined by murder."

"Are you kidding me? This has been great! A dead body, an energy vortex, outdoor yoga, and desert hikes. This has been one of my better vacations. I love crime!"

"I have created a monster." I took a bite of my muffin. It really was good. "How was Lu?"

Juliet's face turned somber. "I think she got food poisoning. Don't tell the chef though. They've had so many bad things happen here this month, the last thing Harmony needs is the health department coming here."

"Shouldn't she see a doctor?"

"I already suggested it, and she threatened to shoot me."

"We'll check on her later. Let's eat breakfast and head into town. We need to get cracking on this case. We leave in less than two days."

"Aye aye, Cap'n Pheesicle!" Juliet saluted.

CHAPTER SEVENTEEN

My eyes were starting to cross, so I squeezed them shut and took a break for a couple of minutes. I was coming up empty on finding anything in the book I had found giving the history of the area. Fortunately, the local newspaper had been digitized and we didn't have to resort to hours of mind numbing searches through reels of microfilm. Juliet had volunteered for the online searches while I combed through the library's historical records and books.

"I found something," Juliet's voice broke through my reverie. I opened my eyes and saw she had a sheaf of papers printed out and a triumphant look in her eye.

"I hope it's good because my brain is starting to hurt."

"There's an old copper mine on the property."

"What? So what's the big deal? Copper mines were all over this area from Jerome to Tucson. Most of the were mined out and abandoned," I said.

"Ah. That is where this gets interesting. Turns out that the Big Moon Copper Mine didn't get mined out. It collapsed back in 1918 and killed five miners."

"I'm listening. It's historically interesting, but I still don't see what it has to do with our dead guy or our prankster."

"Historically interesting because the reason

they didn't reopen the mine is because it's cursed!" Juliet gave me a triumphant whoop causing the reference librarian to cast an evil eye upon us.

"Cursed. Really? You're thinking a curse is what is causing all these bad things to happen at the spa? Oh, how the mighty have fallen. I'll be taking back the crown that says *World's Smartest Sister.*"

"I'm not finished. The reason why they believed it was cursed was because a week before the accident, a Yavapai Indian told the miners that they were poisoning the water and that the ancestors would come back and curse every single one of them. Mine collapses. Miners die. Curse. It all adds up."

"But a curse is causing our mishaps?" I knew Juliet bought into the spirit woo woo with Willow, but I didn't realize how far gone she was. Maybe Wade and I could host some kind of intervention when we got back.

"Not finished. Patience is not your strongest virtue, you know. Maybe Clint and I could have some kind of intervention or retraining when we get back and work on you. Anyway, guess who cursed the miners?"

"Let me guess? Spirit guides?"

"Now you're just being silly. Samuel Riggs."

"Who is?" I asked, still at a loss for what she was saying.

"Idelia Riggs' grandfather."

"Okay. Making it a little clearer than mud. Try enlightening me some more on where you're going with this."

"Here's what I think is going on. Copper is a big-ticket item nowadays. Land that has a copper mine on it would fetch a pretty penny. Idelia Riggs probably heard about the curse as a child from her grandfather and it stuck there. Fast forward years later and she's Francine Whitaker's henchwoman and somehow the story comes back to her, she tells Francine after the land is already sold and the two of them are out of a small fortune. They need to get the land back, but don't have the means to do so. Idelia decides to bring back the curse in a series of misfortunes. Harmony's to down to earth to fall for it, but Steve would be practically falling over himself with fear from a rumored curse."

"But Harmony and Steve haven't mentioned a curse," I protested.

"I don't think Idelia's pulled out the big guns yet. She couldn't reveal the curse without revealing the information about the copper mine. I think they decided to try their luck with ruining their bottom line first because that's the way to get to Harmony. I guarantee you that if Steve and Harmony don't agree to sell, Idelia will have someone let Steve know about the curse."

I thought about Juliet's theory. It was sound. Surprisingly sound, except for one problem. "Idelia and Francine don't have access to staff areas of the spa. How are they causing all the bad things to happen?"

"An insider," Juliet said. "And I think I know who it is thanks to genealogy databases, I found out that someone at the spa is related to Idelia."

"Who?" I was awed by Juliet's detective skills. More importantly, I was awed that she remembered that libraries had databases, and she actually knew how to use them. It brought a tear to my eye.

"Sandy."

"No way. She's so sweet and she likes Steve and Harmony."

"Maybe so, but blood is thicker than spirit water."

Juliet paid for her printouts, and we headed back to the spa to show Harmony and Steve what we found.

When we got back to the spa, we searched for Willow. It was important she heard what we learned, too. I found her lounging next to the pool reading a book on channeling.

"Juliet and I found information at the library we think you and your parents need to hear."

Willow put her book down and stood up. "They should be in their office right now. Mom goes over the books on Fridays in preparation for the weekend."

We headed back inside and to Harmony's office. We found she and Steve sitting side-by-side huddled over a spreadsheet. When Harmony looked up, her face was grim.

"What's the matter, Mom?" Willow asked.

"Things aren't good. We've had cancellations for the upcoming month. I'm sure people don't want to come to the murder spa."

"We may have found something that can help solve at least one of your problems," Juliet said and handed Harmony the printouts from the library.

Harmony started to read through the newspaper article summaries. As she flipped through the pages, she came to the family information and her mouth opened in shock. When she finished reading, she handed the sheaf of papers to Steve and picked up the phone.

"Sandy, can you come down to the office, please." Harmony listened to her response and added, "Finish setting the room up and have Marianne take over. I need to see you right away."

Ten minutes later, Sandy came into the office. She saw us sitting together, and she must have realized that we knew her secret. She burst into tears.

"I'm sorry," Sandy sobbed. "Idelia's my mother's cousin. Money's been so tight and Idelia promised that she would pay my college and give Mama money to help with my sister. I didn't have a choice."

"You always have a choice," Harmony said coldly.

"Now, Honey Bear, she's young and young people make mistakes."

"Steven, she's ruined our business," Harmony bit the words out through her clenched teeth.

"I'll quit. I'll go to the police and tell them about Idelia. I'll do whatever I need to do to make this up to you," Sandy begged.

"You're not going to quit," Steve said.

"What?" Harmony said.

"What?" Juliet and I said at the same time.

"Love of money made Idelia do a horrible thing. Sandy did it because she and her family barely make ends meet. Come on, Honey Bear, you saw the condition of their trailer and you know her mother has health issues. Sandy didn't do this out of meanness or greed."

Harmony sighed and pinched her nose. "You're right."

I felt bad for Sandy after Steve said that. I was fortunate that I had never worried about paying for college and I had always lived in a nice home and had nice things. It made me feel warm and fuzzy inside about Steve. Even if he was a woo woo crystal guy, I liked him.

Steve turned to look at Sandy. "You are going to continue to work here and you're not going to play any more tricks on guests. In addition, Harmony and I will help you pay for your tuition with the understanding that you will maintain a passing grade in all of your classes. Agreed?"

Sandy sniffed. "I don't know what to say. I've

been a jerk to you and messed up your business, put sugar in the gas tank of the Jeep, and you still want to help me? Why?"

"Because a long time ago, I did something stupid and this beautiful lady here gave me a second chance and married me. I'm paying it forward today by having faith in you."

"Wait a minute. What about Brad?" I asked Sandy.

"Brad? I didn't have anything to do with his murder. I swear." Sandy held her hand over her heart. "I don't think Idelia did either. She was as shocked as I was about the murder."

"What are you going to do about Idelia and Francine?" I asked.

"I think once I threaten to report Francine to the real estate licensing board, she and Idelia will leave us alone. The copper mine must be somewhere in the hills behind here. The mine had been buried for over one hundred years and it can stay buried as far as I'm concerned."

"One crime down and one to go," Juliet said. "I am so good."

CHAPTER EIGHTEEN

We left Steve and Harmony talking to Sandy. Willow, Juliet and I went to find Lu. Willow had spotted her earlier with a cup of herbal tea and some toast. I hoped she was on the mend from her food poisoning. I was scared to tell Lu that Sandy was behind it for fear Lu might shoot her.

Lu was by the pool. Her head was back and sunglasses covered her eyes. When we walked up to her but didn't speak, she pulled off her shades and gave us a scary look.

"Are you feeling any better, Lu?" I asked.

"Passable," Lu grunted.

"Food poisoning is brutal," Juliet said. She sat down on the chair next to Lu.

"It's not food poisoning," Lu said quietly.

"Not food poisoning? Ah, crud. Keep your stomach flu away from me," Juliet said and scooted her chair away from Lu's.

"It's not the flu."

"Maybe we should take you to the doctor and figure out what it is before we leave. You don't want to be sick on the road," Willow said.

"Guys," I said, "leave Lu alone. She's not sick." I looked at Lu, and she knew that I knew.

"Not sick, but…" Juliet protested before she fell silent. "Oh."

"Oh," Willow echoed Juliet.

"Oh." Lu laughed. "Oh, my career is over. Oh, my mother's going to kill me. Oh, my boyfriend is going to drop me like a hot potato."

"No, Anthony won't," I said firmly. "He loves you."

"Does he know?" Juliet asked.

"No, and you chuckleheads aren't going to tell him." Lu pointed her finger at us.

"But-"

"But nothing," Lu barked. "This is my decision. Anthony has an amazing career and future. A baby is not in his plans right now."

"I disagree," I said quietly. "Anthony has said he wants a wife and kids."

"Yeah, he does." Lu nodded her head in agreement. "He needs a June Cleaver wife with two point five kids. Not a half Puerto-Rican, half Irish cop who doesn't know how to iron or cook anything more than ramen noodles."

"Isn't that his decision to make?" I asked.

"Anthony's a great guy. He would step up and do the right thing. I love him enough to not make him do it. I broke up with him last night."

Juliet gasped. I sat down in the chair opposite Lu. "Are you sure?"

"I'm sure."

"We'll be there for you," I said. "Clint will be, too."

"Thanks," Lu said. For a moment, I thought she was tearing up, but she looked away and breathed in deeply. "Now go away so I can be sad in peace."

Without another word, we all left the pool area

and went back inside.

"Crap on a cracker, this sucks," Juliet said.

"Yes, it does."

"I'm going to go talk to the spirits and make Lu a charm to protect the baby," Willow said. She hurried off to commune with her guides.

Juliet and I walked slowly over to the lounge, and we both collapsed onto the couch in shock.

"I want to go home," Juliet said.

"Me, too, honey." I hugged Juliet.

"I miss Wade, and I want to hold him and tell him I'll never leave him."

"Me, too."

"Hey! That's my man. Keep your mitts off of him!" Juliet joked.

"I meant I want to tell those things to Clint."

A delivery driver arrived at that moment and interrupted our sister bonding. "Excuse me. I've got a package for a Harriet Konner."

"I don't think there is anyone here by that name," I said.

"It says Harriet Konner in care of Harmonious Healing Spa and Resort," the man in the brown uniform said.

"Maybe it's for a guest who hasn't arrived yet," Juliet said. "Some people mail things they can't take on a plane."

"We'll sign for it and take it into the office."

Juliet signed for the package and set it down on the table in front of her. "What time does our flight leave tomorrow?"

"One o'clock."

"I'm sorry our girls' getaway bit the dust."

"It so bit the dust."

"It crashed, burned and then exploded."

"It not only crashed, burned and exploded, but actually reformed and did it all over again."

"We did help Steve and Harmony out a little," Juliet said.

"We did."

"I got to meet my yoga idol, Hari K'nai."

"You did."

"You managed to only sprain your ankle and not break it."

"I did."

We sat in sisterly silence thinking about our trip. I thought about everything we'd learned about Brad. It wasn't much.

"What have we learned about Brad?" I asked Juliet.

"He was a first-class creep."

"True. We learned that he had a gambling problem and needed money."

"And he cheated on his wife."

"He did."

"He also liked young women, according to Sandy."

"We need to look at the personnel files for the people who were here at the same time as Brad."

"Why?"

"I want to look at the young woman's file who left for college who worked here at the same time as Brad."

I got up and headed back to the office with Juliet close on my heels. I tapped on the office door and Harmony looked up from her paperwork.

"What can I help you girls with?"

"Can we look at the personnel file of the girl who worked here last summer as a maid before she left for college?"

"I can't let you look at personnel files. I could get sued. Those files are confidential."

I knew she was right. I wasn't going to tell her about our midnight escapade. "Can you tell me what the girl's name was?"

"Megan Konner. Why?"

"Do you remember if she was from here or not?"

"I don't think so. If I recall correctly, she was from California. You're being very mysterious. What's this all about?"

"I have one more question. Was she the young girl that Brad was caught with?"

"Yes, she was. She was only eighteen. He should have known better," Harmony said sharply.

"I think I know who killed Brad. Can you call a staff meeting?"

"Sure. Now?"

"If it's not too much trouble, yes. If we meet in the staff break room, that would be great."

Harmony picked up the phone to start calling

the staff. I left her to go bring Lu, Willow and Juliet to the meeting. I was going to have a Hercule Poirot moment. Hopefully, I wouldn't end up with egg on my face.

Thirty minutes later, we were all in the staff room. Sandy still looked scared. Kathy, Bridget, and Louise, who worked part-time in the kitchen, sat together with a man I assumed was the handyman. Hari sat with Marianne, Willow, and Willow's parents. Lu and Juliet sat in chairs near the door.

I stood up and leaned on my crutches. "When trying to solve the murder of Brad Cassidy, I had to consider means, motive and opportunity. That is the key to solving any crime."

Lu coughed, but not before I heard the snort that started it. I cut my eyes at her and she stopped.

"Like I was saying, means, motive and opportunity. First, let's look at means. Brad was killed with a knife in the back. The knife came from the kitchen, so it had to be someone who had access to the kitchen. That is every one of you here today."

"Now hold on," Marianne said, "the police have interrogated me and said they didn't have enough to hold me. I did not kill my ex-husband."

"You're right, Marianne," I said. "You didn't. You did not have the opportunity. Sandy was busy in the spa, so she's off the hook, too."

"Thank you," Sandy sniffled from her seat and some of the fear left her face.

"It was somebody here who hated Brad."

"That's Marianne," Kathy said. She turned to Marianne, "Sorry, love, but it's true. We all thought he was a jerk, but we didn't hate him."

These people were messing up my big reveal. It was so much easier when the suspects sat quietly while Hercule Poirot explained how his little gray cells had solved the crime.

"Ahem," I cleared my throat. "As I was saying, it was someone who hated Brad. Someone whose life had been ruined by him which lets Marianne off the hook. She's doing better with Brad out of her life. She and Manbun-"

"Who?" Marianne asked.

"Sorry. She and Luke are happy and making plans. No. The person whose life was ruined was Megan Konner's. I figured it out when I overheard a telephone conversation between a mother and her pregnant daughter. The mother's voice revealed a great deal of love. A daughter who was clearly in her final month of pregnancy based on what I heard."

I noticed an uncomfortable shifting of everyone throughout the room. I think they knew what I was thinking. "I think Brad got Megan Konner pregnant."

"Maybe so," Willow said, "but Megan's not here. Even if she was, I think it would be hard for a pregnant girl to haul Brad's body into the freezer."

"Megan's not the murderer," I said. "Her mother is."

"This is ridiculous," Hari stood up and turned to Steve and Harmony. "I have things to do and you two are indulging this girl in her child's game of *Clue*."

Lu stood up and moved in front of the door. "I want to hear what she has to say. Please sit down." The tone of Lu's voice stopped Hari in her tracks.

"As I was saying, Megan's mother killed Brad. Here's what I think happened. Megan is a foolish eighteen-year-old girl who loses her head and sleeps with Brad. She gets pregnant, but she doesn't find out until she's already off at college. She contacts Brad and he tells her she's on her own. Brad has more debt than assets. He's just finished a messy divorce where he didn't get the money he expected from Marianne's inheritance. He finds a job in another state.

"Megan is forced to drop out of college. Her mother is devastated. After all, what mother wants her teenage daughter's life ruined by a loser like Brad?"

"Hey, I was married to that loser," Marianne protested weakly. "Not that she isn't right."

"Exactly," I said. "Megan's mother comes here to work like she always does. She doesn't know that Brad has moved out of state. There are a series of mishaps that point to something being off here at the spa. The murderer decides it's the perfect cover. She can murder Brad and the police will tie it to whomever is behind the problems at the spa. She somehow manages to track Brad down and knowing his love of money, offers him some kind of cash incentive to come to Sedona. She lures him into the spa, kills him and stuffs his body into the freezer. She's fit and strong, so moving him is a piece of cake for her."

"That's all well and good," Hari said, "but can you prove it?"

"I think the police will end up matching the prints on the knife to someone here and I'm sure that Megan won't be hard to find."

"Who is Megan's mother?" Steve asked, looking around in confusion.

"Hari K'nai," I said, pointing at her.

"What?" Steve yelped.

"You realize that Hari K'nai can't be her real name? It's Harriet Konner. Hari K'nai is the name she changed it to for business purposes. It sounds so much more exotic than Harriet."

"Well, this has been fun, kids, but I have a class to get ready for. Steven, you really should pay attention to who your daughter hangs around with. They might be a bad influence on her spiritual growth." Hari stood up and pushed her chair under the table.

"Sit down!" Harmony roared.

We all jumped.

Harmony stood up and turned on Hari. "You

wicked, evil woman. You have been floating around here spouting phrases about peace, love, and yoga. You murdered a man and stuffed him in my freezer."

Hari's face was stony. "You don't understand anything. All you care about is your bottom line. It was Brad's karma to die by my hand after he ruined my daughter's future. He was a bad spirit."

"You want to talk about karma?" Harmony asked, then she punched Hari in the nose. "There's your karma."

"Way to go, Mom!" Willow cheered.

Not too shabby for my first big reveal. I think I did Agatha Christie proud.

EPILOGUE

Lu, Juliet and I sat in the airport. Willow had decided to stay and help her parents recover from some of the bad press. Steve was emotionally fragile now that his yogi was a murderer, so Willow thought she and the spirits could help him.

"I can't believe you pulled an Agatha Christie," Juliet said.

"I can't believe it worked," Lu said.

"Me either." I laughed. I had solved a crime and hadn't gotten hurt. The ankle didn't really count.

"She sang like the proverbial canary once she came to," Juliet said.

"We all heard it, so it will stand up in court," Lu said. "Well, done, Phee. You solved two crimes."

"Hey!" Juliet protested. "I figured out the first one."

"Yes, you did," Lu agreed.

"I'm going to wear clothes when I get married," Juliet said, out of the blue.

I laughed and pulled a bar of chocolate out of my purse. "Thank goodness because I really didn't want to have to diet. Clothes hide a multitude of sins."

Lu looked down at her still flat stomach. "I hope so."

ABOUT THE AUTHOR

Amy Lilly grew up in the small town of Cedaredge, Colorado where she spent her free time reading Nancy Drew mysteries and using her Junior Detective Kit to solve mysteries on her family farm. Amy earned a B.A. in English from the University of Iowa and her M.L.S. from SUNY at Buffalo. She spends her free time raising goats, chickens, a herd of well-fed cats and two hyperactive Jack Russell Terriers. She is married with two sons and two beautiful, smart granddaughters and lives in Virginia.

CPSIA information can be obtained
at www.ICGtesting.com
Printed in the USA
LVOW03s1512141217
559733LV00011B/584/P